MR. JUNE

Calendar Boys Series

NICOLE S. GOODIN

Mr. June
Published by Nicole S. Goodin
ISBN: 978-0-9951206-1-7
Copyright 2019 by Nicole S. Goodin
All rights reserved. ©
First published June 2019

Cover design by Nicole Goodin
Images purchased from Deposit Photos
Editing by Spell Bound

For all the babes born in June

CHAPTER ONE

Mack

"Mack, do you copy?" the voice in my earpiece asks again.

I groan and push off the wall I've been peacefully leaning against for the past half hour. "Give it to me one more time, Gilly, I'm hoping I misheard you."

I hear him chuckle. "Don't be like that; she keeps things interesting at least."

Interesting. That's one word for it. I can think of a shit load more colourful ones, none of which will actually help me in the slightest when it comes to removing this particular problem.

"You better get ready, man, the cuckoo is about to fly right into the nest, I repeat, right into the nest."

"Location?" I bark as I round the side of the building.

"North west corner, same as the week before last."

"Someone call security," I mutter.

"You *are* the security, Mack," He replies, clearly amused.

"Well this security needs its own fucking security; this bitch is crazy."

"Maybe you should try spanking that ass." He chuckles.

I grind my teeth together in frustration.

"Go and do something else, Gilly."

"Like what, boss?"

"I don't care. Do literally *anything* other than talk to me," I snap as I approach the north west corner just in time to see a foot with a blood-red high heel on it swinging over the top.

She might be a giant pain in my ass, but I've got to give her credit, I have no idea how she manages to scale *that* fence in *those* shoes.

I cross my arms across my chest and wait, my already-waning patience thinning further.

The other shoe follows, and I let my eyes trail up her legs and over her ass as she lowers herself down over my side of the fence.

There's fuck all to her, and she's got quite a drop to make it to the ground, but I'm not about to offer her a hand down.

She peers down at the ground over her shoulder, her now-orange hair – it was purple last week - blowing in the breeze, before she lets go of her hold and sails to the grass beneath her.

I raise a brow as she lands on the balls of her feet elegantly, and brushes down her black pants before turning, her eyes landing on me instantly.

She pouts when she sees who's here to meet her. "What are *you* doing here?" she demands.

Shit. She's even more beautiful in person than she is on the monitor.

"This is my job, sweetheart. I think a better question is, what are *you* doing here?"

"The *other one* is meant to be on garden duty today." She pushes those big puffy lips out even further, but what's clearly been working on Hugh – the 'other one' she's referring to, isn't going to fly with me, no matter how god damn sexy she looks.

She's going to have to do a hell of a lot better than that.

Weak men are the very reason this little hell raiser is here in the first place, *and* the reason she keeps getting past our defences.

The boss was weak for sleeping with her in the first place, and half the men on my staff are even weaker for letting her distract them with a flash of her thigh or a pout of those lips.

She's nearly breached the house three times in the past month, and that shit is stopping right now, even if I have to get my own hands dirty to make it happen.

"Sorry to inconvenience you," I drawl.

Her eyes drift lazily over my shoulder and past me to the huge building housing the people I'm here to protect.

"Don't even think about it."

"Oops." She smirks and shrugs her dainty shoulders. "Too late."

"He's not here."

She runs her tongue over her bottom lip, a mischievous glint in her eyes.

"Oh, c'mon now, big guy, we both know that's a lie. If *he* wasn't here, *you* wouldn't be either." She takes a step in my direction – a prowl that's designed to make men weak in the knees.

Not me though. It doesn't matter how hot she is, these knees are holding strong, for now at least.

She's right about one thing though. It was a lie. William is right inside. But she's wrong about the last part. Thanks to her, I'm stuck here nearly twenty-four seven, keeping an eye out for her next break-in attempt.

"You want to go back up and over, or is going out the front flavour of the day, fruit loop?"

"Thanks, but I think I'll just pop inside."

I chuckle darkly. "Sure thing, want me to hang up your coat for you?" I ask, sarcasm dripping from my tone.

She narrows her eyes at me and sets her hands on her hips. "You're going to be a problem for me, aren't you?"

"Every god damn day of the week," I reply.

She huffs out a breath. "I'm not going to make it easy for you to get rid of me."

"Wouldn't dream that you would," I drawl.

She pops one of her dark brows at me. "I don't go quietly."

"Oh, believe me, sweetheart. I'm aware. You might not have met me before, but I know *you*, Cristal... and trust me, your reputation precedes you."

She gives me a look, and I can't tell if she's pleased I know how she operates, or if she's pissed about it.

She's about to start, I can feel it.

I count down in my head.

Five, four, three, two, one...

Right on cue, she starts. First, she makes a break for the house, and when I catch her around the waist, the yelling and cursing begins.

"Crazy fucking bitch," I mutter to myself as I sling her over my shoulder, her ass only inches from my face.

I can just imagine Gilly watching on the monitor, howling with laughter I bet. I glance at one of the security cameras and flip the middle finger – just for good measure.

"Put me down, you big hulk!" she screams at me, taking a break from her incessant yelling at the house for a moment.

"Gladly," I announce as I cart her out the now-open front gate and deposit her onto the road side.

She stamps her foot in frustration and glares at me.

"I'll be back, you know that, right?"

"I'm sure you will be," I drawl as I step back inside the gate and watch it close between us. "And just so you know, your crazy is showing."

She considers making a break for it, but she must realise she hasn't got a hope in hell of getting past me because she stays put on her side of the solid iron gate.

"My crazy is *always* showing." She growls in frustration before stomping off down the road, back to that flash-ass, shiny black car she'll have parked somewhere nearby.

It makes no sense. She's clearly not after the boss for the money – it seems she has plenty of that already, from some other poor sucker if I had to guess.

"Gilly," I demand through my mic.

"Mack," he replies, and I can hear in his voice how much he's enjoying this.

"I want an electric wire around the top of the boundary fence... and I want it yesterday."

CHAPTER TWO

Kinsley

I yawn and stretch my hands above my head, my long black hair spilling around me.

I haven't slept that well in weeks. I certainly haven't had dreams like *that* in a long time.

"Good morning, Ms. Barlett."

I glance at my clock. Seven on the dot. Same as every morning.

"Morning, Monica." I yawn again, smiling as I think about my dream, or more importantly the handsome stranger that starred in it.

She pulls open the curtains and light floods into my lavish bedroom.

"The usual for breakfast?" she asks as she ties back the curtains.

I don't feel like fruit and yoghurt this morning. I've got a sudden urge to stuff my face. "How about some pancakes instead?"

"Bacon, maple syrup and blueberries?" she asks as she crosses the room.

I grin at her. "You already know the answer to that; it's not pancakes without it."

"I'll have them ready for you when you come downstairs, Ms. Barlett."

"Thank you, Mon!" I call after her retreating frame.

I've given up asking her to call me Kinsley. You'd think she'd be comfortable with the informality given she virtually raised me when I was a little girl, but nope, always with the official title.

I blame my father. As much as I love him, he's a pompous bastard, and he's *all about* his rules.

I roll out of bed and throw on a deep-blue, silk robe, my toes sinking into the plush carpet.

Everything is so comfortable when you're rich.

I pad across my bedroom and into my perfectly clean bathroom. Everything is always spotless when you're rich too. The perks are endless. I roll my eyes at myself. Internal sarcasm really is wasted.

I arch a perfectly manicured brow at myself in the mirror and comb my fingers through my hair.

I wash my face, pee, and brush my teeth.

Brushing before and after breakfast is a habit that makes no sense, but one I've never been able to shake.

I follow the smell of pancakes downstairs to the kitchen. Monica might be a sucker for the rules too, but she sure knows how to make a killer stack of pancakes.

"Good morning, darling."

"Morning, Daddy." I round the bench and give my father a kiss on the cheek.

He's got a coffee in one hand and the newspaper in the other. Just like every day.

Nothing much ever changes around here.

My father likes things neat, in order, and on a strict routine.

The whole place runs like clockwork, anyone who messes with the king's castle is simply fired and replaced with someone more efficient.

I'm seated no longer than thirty seconds when Monica places the stack of pancakes in front of me and a coffee next to that.

"Thank you, Mon."

Daddy looks at my breakfast choice in question.

I grab a piece of bacon from the top and pop it in my mouth. "Don't worry, Daddy, I'll be back to the healthy option tomorrow."

He strives for perfection in everything – my waist line is no exception.

"What have you got planned for today, darling?"

I resist the urge to roll my eyes. *Absolutely nothing if you had your way,* I think to myself.

Daddy doesn't have a wife, not since my mother screwed things up fifteen years ago, so instead of a trophy wife, he's got me; a *trophy daughter.*

I'm twenty-four years old, I have no qualifications, no career, I still live at home and I'm still expected to call my dad, Daddy, for fuck's sake.

I smile sweetly at him. "I have studio time at ten and I have to meet Jennifer at the charity at three."

It's total bullshit, but he doesn't need to know that.

The only thing I'm encouraged to do are my hobbies and 'passion projects', so if he thinks I'm practising ballet and helping homeless people or whoever with something, then so be it.

I *will* be dancing today, but it sure as hell isn't going to be in a ballet studio. And Jennifer will get her donation, it just won't be hand delivered by me.

"That's wonderful," he says, not even bothering to pull his eyes from the paper in front of him.

I do roll my eyes this time. It's all just so *wonderful*. There goes that internal sarcasm again – so wasted.

I slice into my stack of pancakes and take a bite.

He slugs back the last of his coffee and gets to his feet, tucking the paper under his arm as he goes.

"Don't forget about the charity dinner tonight, Kinsley. I'll have Monica lay out an outfit."

"Thank you, Daddy."

It'll be some flashy, overpriced dress no doubt, with heels, jewellery and shoes to match – I'd bet my inheritance on that.

The trophy daughter will be out in force this evening.

He stops in the doorway and says something in a hushed voice to one of his security team.

I wink at the man in the black suit as my father disappears.

I don't know who he thinks he is – forcing his security to wear suits twenty-four seven, but I do know what he would have said to the goon in the corner.

The orders would have just been given to keep tabs on me. Same as every other day.

My father is a smart man, but he's also a busy one, and he can't see everything that goes on – specifically that I keep his security team's balls in my purse.

I bring another mouthful of pancakes up to my mouth and deliberately make the action slow and seductive as the beefed-up goon watches from across the room.

I smirk as his Adam's apple bobs up and down slowly. He's watching my little show and he likes it.

Men. They're all the god damn same.

I only had to sleep with my father's head of security *once*, not that it was a chore in the least; the man is hot as hell, and now I have the leverage to run this place.

He even so much as thinks about snitching to my father about what I get up to when he's not around, and I spill. Not only would he be fired for bedding the boss's daughter, but he'd probably wind up dead too.

The pathetic excuse for security looks away, subtly trying to rearrange the hard-on he's sporting, and I giggle.

Men.

CHAPTER THREE

Mack

"Gilly, all clear out front?"

"Clear."

"Clear out back too, Mack," Tom chimes in.

I tug at the collar of my jacket, I fucking hate wearing this formal shit, especially when I'm working. It's too restricting, I feel like I've got a hand at my throat.

"Nothing to report in here," I tell them. "Next check in fifteen, over and out."

I'm speaking discretely into a small mic on my wrist, ninety percent of the people in this room would be none the wiser, and the other ten percent are running security in the same way I am.

Boss wouldn't normally require four of us with him to something this heavily guarded, but this Cristal chick is proving to be more resourceful than I would have liked, so security has been upped.

Especially since his wife is here with him tonight.

The man himself – William Wellman – catches my eye, and I nod at him once, letting him know we're all clear, for the moment at least.

Cristal might be crafty, but even she would be doing well to get into this place undetected.

Some of the country's most elite and wealthy are here tonight, and the security team aren't playing around. The only people getting through that door are the ones on the list – no exceptions.

"Mack, do you copy?" I hear Gilly's voice through my ear-piece.

"Copy, what have you got?"

"You're not going to *believe* who the fuck just arrived."

I've told him a thousand times to keep it professional on the radios, but the big dumb bastard never listens.

"Who?" I hiss into my sleeve, doing my best to remain inconspicuous.

"Holy fucking shit, man, you wouldn't read about it. She just got right in. Walked right on in there."

"Gilly, *who* did?"

I raise my eyes to the main door, and there's my answer.

"Shit," I mutter under my breath.

"Get in here, all of you," I demand to my men.

"Copy that."

"On it."

"On the way."

The series of replies come as I spin around to get eyes on the boss. He's still in the same location.

I look back across the room just to make sure I'm not seeing things, but fuck me, it's *her*, and Gilly's right – she's in. Not only did she manage to get in here, but she's actually being welcomed.

She's wearing a bright red dress that is doing wicked things to that lithe body of hers, and her hair, which is now pitch black, is piled on top of her head in a sexy-as-hell way.

She's so fuckable it should be a sin.

It won't stop me throwing her over my shoulder again if I have to, though – nothing stops me from doing my job.

I take a step in her direction at the same moment that my eyes follow up the tuxedo-clad arm of the man she's clinging too.

"Motherfucker," I hiss.

This complicates things... complicates them an awful lot.

That's not just *some guy* she's managed to get to escort her in, it's Kent Barlett; multi-millionaire – billionaire, even... and my boss's biggest rival in business.

He's not even meant to be here tonight – everyone knows that the Wellman's and the Barlett's don't appear in the same circle.

I don't know who the fuck this chick is, but she's good, I'll give her credit for that.

There's not another man in the country that she could have made a bigger statement with.

Kent looks down at the woman on his arm and smiles adoringly before introducing her to the man standing in front of them.

She says something to him and smiles sweetly, like butter wouldn't fucking melt.

My men appear at my side, flanking me, waiting for my instruction.

"Tom, stick close to the boss."

He disappears instantly into the crowd of people.

"Where's Jack?" I ask Gilly.

"Mezzanine." He lifts his eyes skyward and I glance up to see Jack watching carefully from the mezzanine level to our right as though we're controlling a serious threat here.

Maybe we are. Hell if I know.

None of this makes any sense to me. She's just one little woman. Sure, she's full of fire and determination, but the boss has given specific instructions.

'Treat her like a live grenade', he said.

I don't see what the big deal is; so he slept with her a couple of years back or whatever... the chick must be a complete bunny boiler or something.

Even though I think it's ridiculous, I take my job seriously, and if that means protecting my six-foot boss from a five-foot woman, then that's just the way it goes.

"You think she's packin', or what?" Gilly asks.

I shake my head as I watch her carefully.

"No idea. Boss seems awful fucking wary of this one. But she's not here to sell Girl Scout cookies, that's for damn sure."

She glances in our direction as though she can feel the sets of eyes on her.

Recognition dawns on her face and those pouty lips curve up in a devious smile. She raises a delicate hand and waves.

Jesus.

"Go and find Tom in case William and Liana split. I want them covered," I instruct, grinding my teeth together in frustration.

I turn to make sure he heard me, but he's already in motion. Serious situations are about the only time you can count on him to listen to a single thing he's told – even if he is still a total prick on the radios.

I cross my arms across my chest and stare hard as she looks right back at me.

Neither of us is moving, but I know what she's thinking. If *I'm* here, then so is *he*.

Her eyes dart from my face and scan the room, making quick work of locating William and, no doubt, his wife too.

"Fucking bitches be crazy, man," I mumble under my breath.

She tips her head up and whispers something in Kent's ear as she points across the room. He follows her finger, grins deviously and then leads her in the direction she's pointed out.

I already know where they're heading, and I'm moving before I even consciously think about it.

I slip as casually through the crowd as I possibly can, but for a guy my size, it's not an easy task. I get a few scowls, but I don't care, I've got a job to do.

I've got a feeling our grenade could be about to detonate.

I reach the boss before she does and glance around for Gilly. I find him lingering just a few feet away.

I give him the signal to move out.

"Boss," I whisper.

He glances at me and leans his head in towards me.

"She's here."

He leans back away from me, his face paling.

"*Here?*"

I nod. "And so is Kent Barlett."

He pales further.

"What's going on, Will?" Liana – the boss's wife – tugs on his arm.

"Nothing, sweetheart," he reassures her, but he's anything but convincing.

"You've got about five seconds until go time, Mack," Jack's voice comes through my earpiece.

"Mr and Mrs Wellman, I suggest we head out back."

I usher them with my arm, but Liana decides that right now is the moment to stand her ground and ask questions.

"What's going on, Mack?" she demands. "We haven't even had dinner yet."

She's got her perfectly manicured fingers set on her hips now.

"Shit," I mutter to myself.

I know women, so I know for sure that this one isn't going anywhere fast, not until she gets some answers.

"Two seconds," Jack informs me.

"Boss, we've got to go," I tell William.

"Liana, please, we'll talk in the car," he pleads with his wife, but it's too late. The eagle has landed.

"*Wellman*, long time no see."

I know the deep voice belongs to Kent Barlett without even having to turn.

I watch out the corner of my eye as William straightens his spine and turns to face the biggest shark in the business.

He almost gasps when he sees who is on the arm of his most vicious rival.

Poor bastard, I really should have warned him his two biggest fears had come as a package deal.

William glances at me outthe corner of his eye.

"Kent, it's been a while," he manages to say, whilst still sounding relatively composed.

William tugs on his wife's arm and pulls her in closer to him. She shoots him an unimpressed look but complies.

Gilly gives me a 'what the fuck do we do?' look, and I reply with one small shake of my head.

I need a fucking plan.

I still have no idea what this chick wants with my employer, and I'm starting to think I haven't got all the fucking information, given who she's here with.

I'm missing something, and there's nothing I hate more than feeling unprepared.

A grown-ass man shouldn't be shaking in his boots over some woman he fucked forever ago.

I grind my teeth together and look at Cristal – the devil in red.

Fuck's sake, the woman is wearing the shit out of that dress. She's got the attention of half the men in a three-metre radius, and given how beautiful of a woman Liana is, that's a good effort.

She's not paying me one scrap of attention; her focus is solely on William, and she's looking at him the way a cat stalks a bird – as though she intends to end him.

Kent isn't any better. The look in his eye is frightening. It's almost as though he's threatening William with just a glance.

The boss is quite literally shaking in his thousand-dollar shoes, and honestly, it's a little pathetic.

"Shame about that 'Energy Forward' deal," Kent says, his voice arrogant and relaxed – in stark contrast to the gleam in his eyes.

Liana is staring at Cristal, and if looks could kill, the little pain in the ass would have dropped dead by now.

That would have saved me a job at least.

William whispers something to his wife that I don't catch, and Kent's gaze travels down to her as though he's only just noticed she's there.

"Liana, you look as lovely as ever."

She returns his compliment with a glare, and I have to bite back a grin.

Liana has more balls than her husband by the looks of things.

"Trust you to have a woman half your age on your arm, Kent." She tsks at him and fuck it, I do grin.

I'm not the only one; a sly smirk spreads across Kent's face.

"This is Kinsley." He smiles down at the woman on his arm, and my grin drops.

Kinsley?

"My daughter," he continues.

Well I didn't fucking see that coming. Jesus Christ, boss really has got himself into a mess with this one.

"Did he just say *daughter*?" Jack asks, his voice for mine and my team's ears only.

Kinsley – as I now know her – flashes her eyes to me. They're a light sparkling blue – the polar opposite to the dark hell she's causing for me.

She smirks and darts her tongue out to moisten her lips.

I can think of at least a dozen things I could make that pouty mouth good for, but right now, all I'm allowed to do is get my employers out of here.

Credit to boss, he leans in and kisses the side of Kinsley's cheek, but he can't shake that slight tremor.

"Kinsley," Liana addresses her, tone surly.

"I love that dress, Liana, we should chat, leave the men to the business talk," Kinsley suggests.

William's grip tightens on his wife's arm, and he shoots me a look that tells me we need to leave, right now.

I take a step forward. "Mr and Mrs Wellman, we have a situation back at the house, I'm afraid I'll have to escort you out now."

William turns to Kent and his god damn *daughter* and without saying a word, nods, and walks away, tugging Liana with him.

Gilly flanks them immediately, and Tom appears out of thin air to take the other side.

I don't move, my gaze fixed directly on the little problem before me.

She tugs her arm from her father's, who has moved his conversation on to some other poor sucker, and closes the short distance between us.

"Hey, big guy," she rasps into my ear. "You should wear a suit more often, it suits you." Her lips brush my cheek.

I chuckle darkly as she pulls away.

She's good, for an outsider, it would have looked as though she simply greeted me; an old friend perhaps.

I lean in and kiss her cheek in return.

"I'm watching you, *Kinsley*." My voice is gravelly and low, menacing even.

I pull back and turn, not giving her a backwards glance, but if she thought for a second that I wouldn't have eyes on her for the rest of the evening, she'd be wrong.

CHAPTER FOUR

Kinsley

"C'mon now, Hughy, we both know you could get me in there if you really wanted to." I push my chest out a little further, and he groans.

He doesn't even try to hide the fact that he's looking; he's openly staring at my rack.

"I can't, Kinsley... you're going to get me fired." I pout; clearly my name has been updated.

I had no idea William and his wife were going to be there the other night, but what a bonus it was. I haven't been that close to his slime ball of a boss since I was in between his sheets.

I even got to play with that brute who man-handled me the other night... the sexy , arrogant bastard who is very clearly running things around here and telling everyone my real name. Spoil sport.

"I just want *five* minutes," I purr seductively as I run a per-fectly manicured nail down the front of his shirt.

He makes a pained growl, deep in his throat, and that's how I know I've got him.

Men... they're all the damn same.

"Five minutes." He sighs in defeat as his hand snakes out to grip my hip.

I lean in so our lips are a mere millimetre apart. "After you," I whisper.

I step back, his hand dropping as I wait for him to lead the way.

It frustrates me to no end that it's come to this.

I can get inside the property, with little to no problem, in fact. I've even figured out the blind spots in their security feed, but I can never actually get inside the house.

The big guy with the burly arms is always there, or instructing one of his minions to be there, blocking my way.

I *have* to get inside; my window of opportunity is running out, if that electric fence I saw being installed is anything to go by. I'm ballsy, but I'm not insane. Even *I* can't take on a volted wire and win.

Hugh shakes his head, presumably at his own weakness and glances around the side of the building before waving for me to follow.

We make it around that wall.

"Wait here," he instructs, before disappearing around the next corner.

I'll give him thirty seconds before I go after him, I decide.

I get to ten before I'm interrupted.

"Points for trying," a deep voice comes from behind me.

Well fuck.

I turn slowly, doing my best to appear unfazed at what is bound to be yet another failed attempt.

And there he is, the big guy in all his glory.

Huge, sexy bastard...

I should have known it was too easy.

My eyes graze over his jean- and t-shirt-clad body.

The black fabric clings to his torso and arms like a second skin.

I know I told him he should wear a suit more often, but honestly, he looks just as good in this.

He is seriously lickable.

I like to think I'm a woman who's in control of her sexual urges, but there's something about this man that flicks a switch deep inside me.

He smirks at me and prowls in my direction. I'm pinned against the wall of the house before I can even take another breath.

He cages me in with his strong, muscular arms, and I grin.

"If this is what being held prisoner involves around here, then sign me up." I batt my lashes at him seductively.

He chuckles, that same sexy, deep, dark chuckle I heard the other night, and it makes my belly flutter.

"Oh, trust me, *Kinsley*, you couldn't handle being my prisoner."

The way he says my name fills my body with heat.

It's a fucking shame that we've met under these circumstances. If I had met him in the club, I'd have had him by now.

I don't know what story my expressions are telling, but I hear a rumble, right down in his chest.

I gasp as he lifts me effortlessly on top of a half wall, my back roughly hitting the brick behind me.

He shoves my legs apart and forces his way between them, his arms coming down on either side of my hips.

We're pushed so closely together I can feel the pressure from the seam of his jeans pressing against mine.

"You're too fucking sexy for your own good... but you know that already, don't you, Kinsley?" he rasps as he runs his nose from my ear to the base of my throat.

He nips at the skin there, and I swear to god, I'm wet instantly.

His breath is hot on my skin and he smells like a man should; *intoxicating*... strong.

I try to suppress a moan but fail.

He chuckles again, clearly enjoying the torment he's putting me through.

"I could fuck you right here and now, and you'd like it, wouldn't you?"

My head falls back and my eyes close, because *hell yes* I'd like it.

I feel a whoosh of air, and then he's gone.

My eyes snap open.

He's walking away from me, whistling. Fucking *whistling*.

"Now you know how poor Hugh feels when you leave him high and dry," he calls to me over his shoulder. "You really shouldn't use sex as a weapon, Kinsley, you've gotta be smarter than that."

I clench my fists at my sides in frustration.

I got played like a fiddle, but *shit* did he play me well.

"You just gonna leave me out here?" I yell after him.

He stops and turns back to glance lazily at me. "We got a dog, a *big* one... I'm letting him out in five minutes... What you do with that information is up to you."

He smirks at me again before strolling away like he wasn't just part of the hottest moment of my life.

"Fucker," I grumble before I jump down off the ledge and head back for the spot of the garden wall I came over.

He might be joking about the dog, but I'm not taking any chances, not wearing these boots. No mutt is chewing on my designer shoes.

I stomp my way across the lawn.

If he's not watching, one of those other goons will be. I find the nearest security camera and wave at it.

I might have to come up with a new approach to getting what I want, but I won't give up.

They've underestimated what I'm capable of, so maybe it's time I showed them exactly what that is.

CHAPTER FIVE

Mack

I shut the door behind me and lock it for good measure.

That *fucking* woman.

I close my eyes and lean back against the door.

"Hey, Mack?"

I open one eye and glare at him.

"It's getting hot in herre, so take off all your clothes," Gilly sings from the doorway, doing some god-awful attempt at Nelly, and an even worse attempt at a stripper hip thrust.

"Fuck off, Gilly."

"I thought you were going to fuck her right there in the garden." He howls with laughter, ignoring me.

"It's called doing my job, asshole, giving her a taste of her own medicine after she took the bait from Hugh."

"Looked to me like you were getting her all primed up to stick your d—"

"Gilly," I bark. "Fuck. Off."

He chuckles and strolls down the hallway. "So hot in herre," he calls out in his best gangster voice before he disappears.

If I didn't trust that dickhead with my life, I would have fired his ass by now; he's barely worth the hassle.

I stalk off in the direction he went, but I don't follow him into the surveillance room, instead heading up to the second of the three levels of this ridiculously extravagant house.

Rich people have no grip on reality, this place is a joke.

"She's back over the wall, Mack," Gilly calls as he hears me climbing the stairs.

"Let the dog out for good measure," I tell him.

I wasn't kidding about the mutt.

Boss went and picked out the biggest, baddest looking dog he could find after the incident at the charity event.

He's such a pussy.

I rap my knuckles on his office door.

"Come in," he calls.

I swing the door open and step inside.

He eyes me. "She's been back?" he asks, knowing that that's virtually all I report to him these days.

I nod.

"Shut the door."

I do as I'm asked before taking a seat on the far side of his office.

I refuse to sit in one of the low chairs in front of his desk while he sits there on his huge office chair, looking down at me.

He might pay my wage, but he's not my superior, I'm the one who holds his life in my hands most of the time.

William Wellman pisses a lot of people off in business and, quite frankly, in everyday life. He needs me and my team, and he knows it.

"Where is she now?"

"Handled," I answer as I throw my arm over the back of the lounger.

"What's the status on the electric fence?"

"It should be completed by Friday."

He nods. "Good. And the dog?"

"Roaming the yard as we speak – she'll see it."

He glances thoughtfully around the office.

She won't be back here in a hurry. She's a smart woman – I'm not dumb enough to mistake her craziness for lack of intelligence, and she knows she's exhausted her options here at the house.

"You know, one phone call and I could have the police pick her up for trespassing," I offer.

He shakes his head quickly. "I want this handled in-house."

I tip my head and study him.

He's keeping things from me, and nothing fucks me off more.

"Are we just going to keep dancing around the fact that you fucked Kent Barlett's daughter, or what?"

He winces. "I didn't know she was his daughter when I slept with her – it was a long time ago."

She must be about mid-twenties now, so no less than twenty when he decided to put his dick in her – it's not like she was a minor, so I don't understand his reluctance to involve the police, but I don't question it either; it's not my job.

It's his neck on the line, not mine... and if he wants to let some sexy, crazy bombshell cause chaos around him, then that's his choice.

"But you knew before the charity event..." I point out the obvious. He was shocked, but not shocked enough.

"It was brought to my attention, *yes*... she's made her presence known."

"Would have been helpful if you passed that piece of information along there, boss."

He doesn't respond.

"She got something on you or what?"

"Aside from the fact that I fucked my business rival's little girl?" He raises one of his brows at me, as if to say 'isn't that enough?'.

Fair call.

"What does she want?"

He shrugs, his eyes darting out the window as he answers.

He's bullshitting me. She wants *something* from him, or has something over him, and I'd be willing to bet he knows exactly what it is.

"Money?" I take a guess.

He huffs out a laugh. "Did she look like she was short on money?"

She looks the complete opposite; she's practically dripping in it.

"She's really a Barlett?"

"The prized daughter."

"Does Liana know?"

"No," he snaps, "and she's not about to find out either."

I nod my head. So maybe *that's* her angle. I don't really see the point, but my experience with spoilt little rich girls is limited at best.

I just can't figure what she'd have to gain by telling her father, or anyone else for that matter.

I get to my feet. "So, you're just going to hide out in your castle until she gets bored of trying to get to you?"

He shrugs.

"What are you going to do if she tells her daddy?" I smirk, and he glares at me.

"Then I might need you boys to start being armed."

I huff out a laugh as I leave him and his pathetic ass in his office.

If he thinks I'm not already carrying, then he's a fool.

He's also a prick – there's more to this situation than he's letting on, and I don't know how he expects me to do my job properly without having all the facts.

For all I know, he's got an illegitimate child with this crazy bitch, and that's what she's going to expose.

A scandal like that could shake William Wellman's precious kingdom right to the ground.

I trudge down the stairs, mulling it over as I go.

"That's an awfully thoughtful face for someone of your intelligence level," Gilly quips as I enter the surveillance room.

I see Tom try to hide a laugh.

I clip the back of Gilly's head. "That's fucking rich coming from you, Einstein."

I glance over the monitors that display virtually every corner of the interior and exterior of the house.

"Any sign of her?"

"Nope," Tom replies. "But you can bet she sat up there and watched to see if you were bullshitting about that dog, though."

I chuckle. "She should know better than to think I'd bullshit her."

He cranes his neck around to look at me. "So, when you told her you were going to fuck her out there, that wasn't you bullshitting?"

I glance at him out the corner of my eye before going back to scanning the screens.

"I didn't say I was *going to* fuck her, I merely pointed out that if I did, she'd damn well like it."

Both men chuckle, and I grin.

"I'd have liked it too, Mack," Gilly pipes up with a wink. "Nothing like free porn."

CHAPTER SIX

Kinsley

"It's a strip club, Cristal, if you don't *strip*, it kind of defeats the purpose."

"We've been over this, Billy." I raise a brow at him through the mirror in the artificially lit dressing room. "I don't strip. I start off wearing fuck all and I leave wearing fuck all. End of."

"The men want *more*."

"Men always want more. If they could see the goods up there, then they'd be trying to climb inside. It's never enough."

He grimaces at the visual I've just given him.

A gay man running a strip club full of half-naked women; go figure.

He opens his mouth to argue with me further, but I cut him off.

"You know the deal, Billy, I'm not a stripper – power to those ladies with their tatas out up there, but it's not me. I'm here for inspiration, and you make a killing from me, whether I strip or not."

He goes to speak again, but I hold up a finger, silencing him. "Now you can either stop hounding me to get nude, or I can walk. We both know this isn't a long-term thing anyway, but if you want to call quits on that pretty little stream of cash I'm bringing in for you right now, you just say the word, cupcake."

He sighs – he lost this battle before it even began.

"That's what I thought." I smirk.

"Alright, Cristal." He shrugs. "You win."

He knows it's not my real name, but he's smart enough not to ask for it at least.

This arrangement we have, temporary as it is, benefits him greatly – he's got throngs of men that come in here asking specifically for me.

I don't take a cent from him either, I share my tips out to the other girls after Billy takes his cut, and he doesn't pay me a wage to dance.

I'm only here to better my dancing. I needed more sex appeal, and what better way to get it than dancing in a strip club.

Plus, I kind of like the attention. Just a little bit. A man worshipping at your feet isn't the worst thing in the world.

"You ready to get back out there then?"

I giggle. "Oh please, you should know I'm always ready." I rise from my chair and strut past him. "Show time, Billy."

***

"Again," I tell the skinny young dude in the corner who controls the music.

The beat pulses through the room, and I start my routine all over again from the beginning.

"That's good, Kinsley, much better. Whatever you've been doing, it's working," my dance teacher praises me when the track ends.

I've studied dance my whole life – ballet when I was a child and a teenager, with hip hop and jazz classes snuck in when my father was too busy to notice.

I still do the odd ballet class here and there to keep up appearances for Daddy, but my true dance style would have his jaw dropping.

I'm more comfortable dancing in the ghetto with a crew of misfits than I am in some fancy studio on the east side.

Unlike most of the people I hang with though, I do both.

This isn't just a bit of fun for me. One day I want to dance and choreograph for a living, not that my father would ever approve, but one day that won't matter either... He can't keep me locked in his castle my whole life.

I smile at her, but her praise isn't enough for me, I need to know *myself* that it's perfect.

"That's all for today. I want you to work on the turn in the second section, but other than that, it's great, Kinsley, really... sultry, sexy and natural."

"Thanks, Mrs. T."

I grab my bag on the way out and press the button on my key to unlock my sleek black Audi, stripping off the long sleeve covering I wear over my arms and shoulders to cover my tattoos as I go.

I get several disapproving looks from the prim and proper ballerinas waiting out front – for their minivan-driving mummies, no doubt.

I'm an enigma to most people around here; no one can really figure me out.

I slide in the car and toss my bag onto the seat next to me. I start the engine and peel out of the car park, their uptight scowls following me.

I head for the big house that I haven't been able to get near in weeks.

I drive past slowly, taking it in. The electric fence is still in place around the top of the stone wall, and I get a glimpse of the huge Rottweiler strolling around the side of the house.

"Well played, big guy, well played," I mutter to myself.

While I didn't account for this in my plans, I think eventually it'll work in my favour. William and his pretty little wife can't hide in their mansion forever, and when they decide that I've finally given up, and they do come out, I'll be waiting.

CHAPTER SEVEN

Mack

"It's been nearly a month, Gilly. She hasn't been back."

"You say that like it's a bad thing?"

I scowl at the monitor in front of me. It's not over. It can't be.

He claps me on the shoulder. "Relax, big man, the little fruit cake has moved on, and as much as I miss checking out her security footage, this is a win. Some might even say you're good at your job."

I huff out a humourless laugh. It's because I'm fucking good at my job that I'm concerned.

Kinsley has an agenda; that much is painstakingly obvious. What that agenda is, however, is no clearer now than it was the last time she was here.

I hate to admit it, but I'm almost bored without her antics to keep me busy.

"If I thought she'd really given up, then I'd relax."

"Like you said, it's been weeks... *chill.*" He spins his chair around, his back to the monitors. "Are you ready for tonight?"

I'm so far from 'ready for tonight', it's almost laughable.

Tom's getting married next week, and tonight is his bachelor party.

Jack and Hugh drew the short straws and are working tonight, while the rest of us will be joining the 'fun'.

I tried to switch with both of them, but Gilly wasn't having it. According to him, I 'never go out anymore', and I was 'fucking attending' even if he had to drag me there himself.

So now I'm facing an evening consisting of what I assume will be drinks poured too strong and woman wearing not nearly enough.

"Smile, Mack, there will be strippers."

He grins like a little kid on Christmas, and I'd be willing to bet that I'll have to get him out of trouble at one point or another before this night is over.

It's one of the 'perks' of being friends with a guy like Scott Gilbert.

"You need a rum." He points at me before flying out of his chair and heading for the door.

I shake my head – this is going to be a long fucking night.

"You coming or what, chuckles?" he calls out to me when I don't follow.

I groan.

"You better improve your mood, bro, you'll scare off all the pussy."

"Fuck my life," I mutter to myself as I get to my feet.

***

"I fucking *told you* there would be strippers." Gilly rubs his hands together in anticipation as we walk in the door of the upmarket strip club.

It could be worse I guess, we could have gone down town to one of the really skanky ones.

"Give it up for my girl, Dee Dee."

I snort at the name. It doesn't matter if you're in an upmarket joint or not, the girls always have stripper names like Candy and Mindy.

"Up next we have the crowd favourite, Cristal, and damn does she look fine tonight."

Cristal, Sapphire, Destiny...

Gilly punches my arm. "C'mon, bro, we're going VIP."

I follow the group of drunk men over to the three more private booths on the opposite side of the stage and slide into one with Gilly, Tom, and one of his mates whose name I forgot, who is so drunk he's virtually passed out.

Gilly pulls a stack of notes out of his pocket and waves them in the air. "Wonder what *Cristal* has for us, boys."

I order a rum on the rocks from the topless woman and before I know it, she's back with my drink.

She winks at me as she places it on the table. I let my eyes rake over her bare tits – that's what she's got them out for anyway – and I sit back, taking a mouthful of my drink as she walks away, an obvious sway in her hips.

I'm nowhere near drunk enough for this shit.

The music starts and Gilly starts whooping and cheering.

A woman struts onto the dark stage, only her silhouette visible.

The beat pulses through the room, and I glance around the crowd. Men that looked bored before are now sitting up at attention.

Cristal really is the crowd favourite.

I chuckle to myself; I bet this chick has nothing on the woman I knew as Cristal.

The light hits the woman of the moment and the word 'fuck' falls from my lips.

"Is that...?" Gilly asks at the same moment Tom utters, "No fucking way."

The crowd erupts into cheers and cat calls as she moves to the beat, shaking her ass in those tiny little shorts.

"Kinsley," I growl.

It's *her*, and fuck she looks sexy. This crowd has good taste – she's not even exposing herself yet, and she's got more sex appeal than every one of the topless waitresses wandering around.

Her long black hair is loose, spilling over her bare shoulders and barely-covered body. She moves like she was made to dance.

"Jesus Christ," Gilly groans. "You should have fucked her when you had the chance, Mack. Fucking hell, *look* at her."

He doesn't need to tell me, I'm *looking* at her, everything from those fuckable lips to that tiny little waist and the tattoos scattered across her body that I've never seen before.

The woman is a walking wet dream, but I get the feeling she'd be more of a nightmare than a dream when it really came down to it.

"What the fuck is billionaire Kent Barlett's daughter doing stripping?" Tom hisses at me.

A mighty fine fucking question that is. I bet her daddy doesn't know his pretty little girl is down here taking her clothes off for money.

"In her defence... she's not *technically* stripping," Gilly replies, his eyes glued to the woman on the stage.

Her song ends and someone from the other side of the stage yells out to her, "Take it off, baby!"

The stage is engulfed in darkness once again, and I hear her giggle float through the room.

When the lights come back on, she's gone.

I chug back the rest of my drink and look between my two guys. "Did I just fucking imagine that?"

Gilly chuckles and shakes his head. "My hard-on says otherwise."

"You're sick." Tom laughs at him, shoving his shoulder.

"At least we know she's not breaking into boss's house while we're out," Gilly offers with a shrug.

"I wonder what the fuck that's all about..." Tom muses.

I get to my feet.

"Where are you going?" Gilly demands.

I raise a brow at him. "To go and find out what the fuck that was all about," I reply, as though it's the most obvious thing in the world.

I sweep the room for the guy I saw earlier – the one who was trying to blend in, but who is clearly the boss here.

I find him at the bar. "Hey, boss man." I nod at him.

His brows shoot up in surprise. "Who, *me*?"

"Save it." I smirk at him. Half the guys in here might be too pissed to notice who runs the show, but not me. "That last chick." I glance at the stage she was on, that now has some half-naked chick that Gilly is throwing money at. "*Cristal*... I want a private dance."

He shakes his head. "Cristal doesn't do private dances."

"I'll give you two grand for five minutes with her."

His eyes bulge. "Give me a minute."

He disappears around the bar and out back. I consider following him but decide against it.

He'll be back. Money talks... I'll get some answers from her, whether she likes it or not. I'll get a lap dance while I'm at it too, because why the fuck not – I'm paying for it.

She might be crazy, but she's also hot as hell.

I order another drink while I wait, and just as the bartender hands it to me, the boss man comes back.

"If you'll follow me out back, sir, I can't have the regulars seeing you with Cristal out here on the floor."

I nod at him and pick up my drink. I expect him to take me through the way he just went, but instead, he takes me to the other end of the bar and through a door that he shuts behind us.

"Third door on the right," he instructs.

I reach into my pocket and pull out a stack of hundreds. I press them into his hand and head down the hall.

"Pleasure doing business with you, sir," he says.

I don't turn back.

I reach the third door and turn the handle.

The room is empty other than a couch and small table. It's only dimly lit.

I shut the door behind me and take a seat on the couch.

I'm only waiting about thirty seconds before I hear the door handle jostle.

I have to give credit to the awkward little man who brought me down here, he runs an efficient ship.

She slips into the room, facing the door as she shuts it softly behind her.

"You must have paid a lot for this."

"Worth every cent," I reply.

She turns and as her gaze lands on me, recognition dawns.

Her eyes widen slightly in surprise, and I wait in anticipation to see what she's going to do next, because when it comes to this particular woman, I'm never quite sure.

A devilish smile curves up the corners of her full lips. "You miss me, big guy?"

"Something like that." I smirk at her as she crosses the small room towards me.

She drops into my lap, her hands weaving into my hair and my hands grip her hips on instinct.

"I missed you too," she purrs in my ear.

She grinds in my lap for a bit, and fuck it feels good – she's got skills.

"So, what did you really bring me back here for?" she asks after a few moments.

I run my hands up the skin on her bare back. "I was curious."

She spins and parks her sexy ass right on the spot where my dick is straining against my jeans. "*About?*"

I grab her hair and pull her back against me, so I can speak in her ear. "What a billionaire's daughter is doing dancing in a strip club," I growl in her ear.

I release my hold on her silky black hair and she spins again so she's straddling me, her knees on either side of my hips.

She lifts her ass so her cleavage is right in my face, but I don't look down, instead training my gaze on her light blue eyes.

"You have pretty eyes."

She sinks back down and grinds against me. "Thank you, and I'm doing just that, *dancing*."

I lean in and brush my lips against the skin under her ear; she stills and tips her head back to allow me easier access.

"You're a gorgeous woman, Kinsley," I murmur as I trail kisses down her neck to her throat.

Her hands are back in my hair, gripping on to me. I'm pretty sure this isn't part of what I paid for, but I'm not about to start complaining.

"I want to fuck you so badly it hurts," I admit.

"What's stopping you then, big guy?" she asks, her breath coming in heavy pants. She wants me too.

I nip at her throat and pull away. "I don't have all the facts. I can't fuck you without all the facts."

I don't even know why I'm here anymore – I can't tell if I'm thinking with my head or my dick.

I fucking want her, but I won't let it stop me from doing my job, that's the only thing I know for certain. I might fuck her, but it won't stop me from taking her down if I have to.

"I met your boss here you know," she says as she continues grinding against my now rock-hard dick.

That explains why he called her Cristal then.

"He picked you up in a strip joint? Classy."

She giggles. "Says the guy getting a lap dance."

"It's for research purposes." I smirk.

"Research *this*," she whispers as she drags my face to hers.

Our lips collide in a frenzy of passion and lust.

I want this sexy fucking woman more than I want anything else.

She tugs my bottom lip between her teeth, and I growl deep in the back of my throat.

I'm not stupid enough to think there's no cameras inside this room, but I am stupid enough to not give a fuck.

"What do you want with the boss?" I murmur against her lips.

She giggles and pulls back so she can look into my eyes. "C'mon now, big guy, you know I'm not going to just give up all my secrets."

I know she won't. That would be too easy.

I chuckle darkly and drag her back to me.

There's a firm knock at the door. "Time's up, Cristal."

She releases a deep breath against my mouth, it feels like disappointment.

"Guess the boss man doesn't like me playing with his toys."

She leans back, but I don't let go of my hold on her.

"I'm nobody's toy."

There's another knock at the door.

"Sounds like you better go."

I let my hands fall to my sides and she stands, eyeing my obvious erection as she goes.

"Sorry I couldn't take care of that for you." She smirks.

I shrug.

"It was good to see you, big guy, we should do this again."

I spread my arms across the back of the couch and watch her as she walks to the door.

We'll be doing this again alright; I just won't be paying two grand to do it.

She rests her hand on the door handle and glances back at me over her shoulder. "And I'm not a stripper... you need to learn that things aren't always as they appear."

She leaves the room, and I consider her words as I readjust my hard-on.

Chick is crazy – I literally just saw her dance in a strip club – she just got all up in my junk for the past five minutes... I'm pretty confident she *is* in fact a stripper, despite the fact that she doesn't need the money and didn't actually take any clothes off.

I just can't figure this woman out.

Sex appeal for days.

Tempting as fuck.

Crazy as shit.

What a god damn *lethal* combination.

CHAPTER EIGHT

Kinsley

"Jared McKenzie, huh?"

"Yes, ma'am."

"You're sure?"

"Big fella, tattoos on one arm?"

"Sounds about right." I nod.

"He's your guy then. They call him Mack."

"Thank you, Steven; you've been more than helpful."

"It's Shaun," he corrects.

"I don't care." I dismiss him with a wave of my hand.

Jared McKenzie... of course he has to have a hot guy name. He couldn't have had a name like Nigel or Eugene.

No, he's got a strong name. It suits him, fuck it all.

That man is too fucking hot for his own good, or maybe for *my* own good. He's a distraction I don't need... but I kind of like the guy – he doesn't put up with my shit... he admits when he wants me. I'm not used to men being so straight up... unless of course he's just playing me at my own game.

He's not likely to want me after I finally get this thing done and out there in the world, thanks to him and those other goons, I'm going to have to get more creative.

It's potentially going to cause problems for me that Jared McKenzie has discovered my little side gig at the strip club. If he decides to run to my father and spill his guts, I'm going to find myself in a *world* of trouble.

I can't think too much about that right now though, I've got bigger fish to fry.

One specific fish to be exact – a real slimy one called William Wellman.

***

I tuck my brand-new yoga mat under my arm and glance around the room.

I've never understood yoga – it's not that I'm not flexible enough, because trust me, I most certainly am, it's all the breathing in and out shit that gets me.

It's so *peaceful*... not at all me. Personally, I prefer chaos.

I glance at the blonde woman on the far side of the room, laughing and joking with a couple of her girlfriends.

She's a beautiful woman, and she's probably lovely too – but unfortunately for her, she married the wrong man... so, no matter how pretty or nice she is, it's still irrelevant.

At least she's had the balls to leave the house, unlike her piece of crap husband, who is still hiding in his mansion.

It's been a whole month since I last attempted to break in there, but the guy is still shaking in his designer boots.

He'll have to come out soon though; he's got a deal to close, and he can't do that in sweat pants from his couch. Not that I care much about what he does.

I roll out my mat and sit down on it, still watching the woman I came here to see.

Most of the women start stretching, so I do the same – I want to blend in.

I steal glances at her across the room as I manoeuvre my body into positions that would make most women cringe to merely think about.

"As impressive as that flexibility is, I don't think you're here for the yoga." A deep voice behind me stills my stretching.

I don't need to turn to know it's the big guy... *Mack*.

"Shit," I mutter under my breath.

I was *sure* she'd come out without security.

One of her friends brought her here in their car, but I didn't see anyone tail them, or me for that matter.

"I saw you around the corner from the house in that shiny black car." His voice is closer to my ear now, so close, in fact, that I can feel his breath on my neck. "I saw you before you even woke up this morning, Kinsley."

I shudder. I can't help it, his words seduce me, even if that's not his intention.

I know my plan has gone to shit, and I know he's probably going to punish me for getting this far, but all of that is over-shadowed by the desperate need I have to press my lips against his again.

Despite all warning from my brain telling me that it's not a good thing he's so many steps ahead of me, I *like* the fact that he's been watching me.

"I have to admit, I'm impressed... going after the boss's wife, because he's too much of a pussy to leave the house..."

My lips turn up into a smirk.

He *is* a fucking pussy.

"But you didn't account for me... it's time to go," he rasps in my ear.

"But yoga is just about to start." I pout.

"Don't pretend you give a fuck about yoga, Kinsley."

I both hate and love that he knows I couldn't care less about this class, but I still don't move.

"We can do this quietly, or we can do this full noise – your call."

I huff out a breath as I contemplate my options.

I glance over at Liana Wellman again, and she's staring right back at me, her forehead etched in a frown.

I could just yell it across the room at her, but I see now that it wouldn't have the desired effect. I should have known that this plan was never going to be successful – annoyingly handsome bodyguard in the way or not. If I do this here and now, I'll be put down as being crazy.

"Fine, I'll go quietly," I grumble as I get gracefully to my feet. "But you're carrying my mat, *Jared McKenzie.*"

He raises a brow at me in surprise as I lay eyes on him for the first time since we basically dry fucked, and *Jesus*... he's as mouth-watering as ever.

"You're not the only one capable of doing some digging, big guy."

I stomp off my mat and in the direction of the door.

Out the corner of my eye, I see him bend down and snag my mat off the ground. I smirk.

"Sorry to rush off," I call to the instructor, "protective boyfriend." I tip my head to the huge man who's now caught up to me and roll my eyes.

He grabs my arm and tows me out. "That's just fucking great, fruit loop, really fucking great."

I pull my arm from his grip and smirk at him. "Oh, poor little Jared... you should know by now that I *never* go quietly."

He ignores me, and points at a massive tinted-out black Land Rover. "Get in."

I stop and sit my hands on my hips, popping a brow at him. "What the fuck for?"

He stops rounding the hood of the car and brings his wrist up to his mouth. He mutters something I can't make out.

"I've got one of my men watching Liana. You're not getting near her, so you may as well get that sexy fucking ass in my car and do as you're told for once in your life."

I smirk at him. "You think my ass is sexy?"

"Unbelievably fucking sexy," he growls, and I feel his words crawl up my spine.

He turns, no longer waiting for me, and climbs into his vehicle.

I glare at the blacked-out window for a moment.

I contemplate making a break back into the yoga studio, but I doubt he's joking – she'll be protected, and there was something he said that's made me curious about him, so against my better judgement, I open the door and climb in.

He looks over his shoulder at me as I settle in the back seat. "Really? What the hell do you think this is? A taxi?"

"I dunno what this is, big guy, I'm just along for the ride."

"Get back out and get in the front," he demands, and god he's hot when he's bossy.

I shake my head in refusal.

He growls. Actually freakin' growls. "*Kinsley*," he warns.

I smirk and slide through the middle of the front seats until my ass lands where he wants it with a soft thud.

"Can we go now? Or do I have to suck your dick to get this thing started?" I drawl.

He glances at me, grins and starts the engine. It purrs to life.

I don't know where we're going, for all I know he's taking me straight to the police station to have me arrested for stalking, but for some reason, I'm incredibly unfazed.

There's a chance we're going somewhere private for a repeat of the other night, so this little excursion is a risk I'm willing to take.

We weave through traffic like we're in a sleek sports car and not a huge big tank-like four-wheel drive, and honestly, I'm a little impressed.

Every so often, he glances at me, shakes his head, and goes back to looking at the road.

"So, where are we going, big guy?" I clasp my hands together over my tight leggings.

"I should be taking you home to your father and finding out if he's aware that his precious little girl is shaking her ass for money."

I gesture for him to go ahead and do it, while I hope like hell that he doesn't call my bluff. I don't need my father knowing my business, and if he discovers that there's a gaping hole in his security, then he'll fire them all, and I'll have to start this whole process from scratch – and god only knows what the new guy might look like... I'm not sure I'd have it in me to screw an ugly old dude.

He chuckles. "You've got a real set of balls on you, woman."

He eyes the road again before coming to a stop on the side of a quiet street. I don't look – that's what he wants me to do.

"Do you drink coffee?"

"I've had three already this morning," I inform him.

"May as well make it four then."

CHAPTER NINE

Mack

"I'd have picked you for a mocha soy latte with extra foam kind of girl," I say as I pass her the black coffee she ordered.

She takes the cup from me, her hand brushing mine, and shakes her head. "First off, that's not even a thing, and secondly, what makes you think you know me at all?"

"I think I might know you just a little bit." I chuckle, thinking about the way she rubbed herself all over my crotch.

"You think you do. But you only see what I let you see."

I shake my head at her and watch as her crystal blue eyes search my face. "I see *everything*, whether you like it or not."

She shifts in her seat, I'm making her nervous, or turned on – I can't figure out which of the two.

"Why'd you bring me here?"

She sips on her drink, and I envy that cup; lips have never tasted so sweet.

"Keep you out of trouble."

She gives me a look that screams nothing but trouble. "Good luck with *that*." She smirks deviously.

I thought the same thing.

My phone buzzes in my pocket and I bring it up to my ear without bothering to look at who's calling.

"Mack," I say.

"Is Tom pulling my dick or did you seriously put that little hell raiser in your car and whisk her away?" Gilly demands.

I glance at Kinsley and she's grinning wide enough for me to know that she heard every word he's just said.

"I don't know what you and Tom are doing with your dicks, but yes, I have her with me. The situation is under control."

"What's your location?"

I bark out the address even though he could look up my location himself on the GPS tracker in about thirty seconds.

I hear him tapping it into the system.

"You're taking her for *coffee*? Are you fucking dating this chick or what?"

"It's a coffee, Gilly, I'm not fucking her on the counter."

Kinsley giggles and covers her mouth with one of her hands.

"She must have a magic pussy or something, dude, because you have lost your god damn mind, and coming from me, that's really saying something."

"What the fuck do you want, Gilly?" I demand.

"Don't touch the voodoo v-jay-jay, man, it's not worth it," he warns me.

"I'm hanging up."

"Make good choices!" he yells before I hit end on the call.

Magic pussy. I scoff as I toss my phone on the table.

I've really got to start screening my calls.

"He sounds fun." She waggles her brows at me. "How do I get *him* to be my new babysitter?"

"I'm not your babysitter," I say, even though that's exactly what I am right now.

She pouts before licking her lips, and my dick jumps.

This attraction is becoming a real problem.

I don't know what I was thinking taking her out of there, or more to the point, taking her with *me*.

I should have deposited her back at her fancy-ass car once I got word that we were clear, and then moved on with my day.

"Can we cut the bullshit and the games for a minute?" I ask.

She sips her coffee and sets the cup down on the table in front of her. "By all means."

"What the fuck are you doing, Kinsley? This obsession you have with William... what the hell is it all about?"

She laughs humourlessly. "I'm not *obsessed* with him."

"Aren't you? Because from where I'm sitting, trying repeatedly to break into a man's home gives a pretty clear impression of being obsessed."

She gives me a sly smile. "I've told you, Jared, things aren't always as they appear."

Nobody calls me Jared anymore except my mother, I've been Mack since I was ten years old, but coming from her mouth, Jared works.

"Why don't you save us both some time and tell me how things really are then?"

"No can do, I'm afraid, big guy."

"You're a real pain in my ass, you know that, right?"

"I think that's why you like me so much."

I bring my coffee to my lips and swallow a mouthful. "I can't touch you while you're causing problems for the boss."

"That's not what you said the other night."

I chuckle darkly – she's not wrong, and that brings me to my next question. "Why are you dancing in a strip club?"

She runs the tip of her finger around the rim of her cup, and I can almost feel it on my fucking skin.

This woman is messing with my head.

Maybe Gilly was right and she does have some kind of magic pussy after all.

"My dance teacher told me I needed more sex appeal."

So she's a dancer... and her teacher must be blind.

"I find that hard to believe."

The woman is literally dripping in sex appeal. I'm not sure she could do anything without looking sexy, even if she tried.

She shrugs and for the briefest flash of a second, I see vulnerability in her eyes. It's gone as fast as it came.

"I dance at the club for *inspiration*. Not for money or sex or whatever else you've conjured up in your mind."

"Are lap dances part of the package?" I smirk.

"Only for you, big guy." She winks.

"So you're a dancer."

"It's the only thing I really give a shit about."

"Other than breaking and entering," I offer.

She rolls her eyes and grins. "That's just a means to an end."

I wish I knew what that fucking end was.

"What kind of dancing do you do?"

"If you asked my father, classical ballet."

"I'm not asking your father," I rasp.

She pauses her finger for a second before going back to running circles around the rim of the cup.

"Hip hop... freestyle..." She shrugs. "I don't really know how to define the style of dance that I do best."

"So that's what you do then, you're a dancer?"

"I'm not *anything* when it comes down to it... I'm a trust fund baby. I'm whatever I'm told to be."

"Like fuck you are."

My words swirl in the air between us as she takes another sip of her drink.

"You think you've got me all figured out?"

I frown. "I couldn't be further from having you figured out, and just so you know, it's driving me crazy."

"Good." She smirks.

I know that me being here with her serves a purpose for my job – it gives the boss time to go out and meet clients without feeling like he's got to look over his shoulder, but I'd be lying if I said I was hating it.

She's an intriguing woman.

"So..." she asks, clasping her hands together and leaning forward towards me. "How long do you have to keep me here for? William must be about done in that meeting."

How the fuck...

I cock a brow at her in question and she giggles gleefully.

"Oh please, we both know this isn't a social visit, no matter how much we both might enjoy another one of those."

I chuckle. "Hey, I didn't have to bring you for coffee. I could have made you sit in the car with the window cracked for the past half an hour."

She rolls her eyes and glances at her watch. "But seriously... can I go? Yoga is over now, Liana will be on her way home, and even if I tried to get all the way across town to where William is, I'd never make it in time to catch him. You're free and clear, big guy, and I've got shit to do."

I study her as she flips her long dark hair over her shoulder and glances around the coffee shop. I don't know how she knows any of this... where Liana does yoga... where William does business...

"Should I be concerned about a leak in my security team?" I question her.

She shakes her head, amusement dancing in her eyes. "No, but my father should be *very* concerned about the state of his."

The woman is smart, I've got to give her that. She's also ballsy as hell; I doubt a man like Kent Barlett would be all too happy about his security team being used for her personal vendetta. Although, given the toxic relationship between my boss and her father, maybe he wouldn't give a shit after all.

"Does your father know you're running around town, scaling fences and stalking rich men?"

"What do you think?"

"Does he not have his team following you?"

"He thinks he does." She pops one shoulder. "According to Daddy's security, I'm meeting with a woman from a charity at one, and I've been to ballet class this morning."

"Why lie?"

"It's just easier that way."

"Easier for who?"

"Him... me... I dunno. I'm all he's got – it's easier for us both if he thinks I'm the perfect daughter."

"Where's your mum?"

She raises her brows. "Coming in with all the tough questions, huh, big guy? Careful, someone might go thinking we were friends."

Friends is the last thing I'm worried about anyone thinking we are.

"You didn't answer the question."

She hesitates, but eventually answers, "She left when I was nine – I haven't seen her since. She's been gone fifteen years now."

"I'm sorry."

"Don't be. She was a cheat. She broke my father's heart and then thought he'd let her stay... you might think my morals are all messed up, but I have no patience for cheating – it's about the only thing my father and I have in common."

I don't know what to say to that, but I don't get a chance to respond anyway. She glances at her watch again before getting to her feet. "Can you take me back now? I really do have things to do."

I nod once and stand.

I follow the sway of her hips to the door.

"You sure you don't want to fuck me on the counter before we leave?" she asks, her brow raised and her tone sassy.

I hold the door open for her and she brushes past me. "Don't make offers you have no intention of following through with," I growl in her ear.

She laughs, her head tipping back, letting her hair fall down to her ass.

Tempting... so fucking tempting.

CHAPTER TEN

Kinsley

I know he's following me.

He's been doing it all day – I don't think he's even attempting to hide the fact the he's behind me anymore.

That big black four-wheel drive has been on my tail for hours – ever since he returned me to my vehicle, to be exact.

I smirk to myself. I hope Jared McKenzie is accustomed to the south side, because shit is about to get pretty ghetto. He's in for a real treat out here tonight.

I glance over my shoulder as I slide out of my car, and sure enough, the big black vehicle is pulling in just a few spaces down.

I wave out to him and laugh to myself at the unexpected direction my evening has taken.

I lock my car and stroll off down the street. I've got to walk a little way; you can't bring a car like that into a place like this and expect it to go down well, so I usually park a few blocks away.

I glance down at my beat-up pair of vans and cut-off denim shorts. The evening dress and heels I left the house in are tossed in the back seat of my car, waiting for me to get back and put them on again... it's *all* about appearances after all.

My father doesn't even know I own clothes like the one's I'm wearing right now. He'd probably have a heart attack if he saw me wearing these, but I like to blend in, and I can't do that in a three-thousand-dollar pair of shoes.

I hear the pounding beat in the distance, and I pick up my pace. I hope the big guy is prepared to move fast – he's going to have to be if he thinks he's going to keep up with me.

I jog down the final block and turn the corner, searching instantly through the crowd for the bright red hair that I know will be here.

Courtney is the only person in my life I'd consider a real friend – and she's not even close to being the type of person I'm allowed to spend time with in public.

My father would have a shit fit if he knew I spent countless evenings in darkened streets with a woman who has more piercings than I can count.

I jump up onto a concrete pillar and glance around the crowded cul-de-sac; there's got to be about two hundred people out here.

I spot Court on the other side of the group and jump down.

I can feel eyes on my back, so I assume Jared has followed me – right here into the thick of it.

That makes me grin.

He wanted to know what type of dance I like... *well*, he's about to find out.

I push my way through the throngs of people until I find Courtney and a few of the guys from our crew.

"K! You made it!" she shrieks as she pushes past one of them to hug me.

The guys raise their chins to me in welcome.

I laugh as she squeezes me tight. "It's packed," I breathe as she finally releases me.

"*Everybody* came out tonight. I'm so glad you're here, I have some new stuff I want to go over with you."

Court is strictly a street dancer – she's had no formal training whatsoever and that's what I love most about her style – it's one hundred percent her, the only downside is that she struggles with choreography.

That's where I come in.

I love to dance but planning a routine... thinking through the steps...that's something I could see myself doing with my life – if I had a normal life that is.

"Babe." She leans in and hisses at me. "Don't look, but there's a hotty over there *staring* at you."

I shake my head in amusement. "Big guy?"

"Like 'I could toss you around the bedroom no problem at all' kinda big." She nods.

"He's a bodyguard," I explain with a roll of my eyes.

Her eyes widen. "You brought your *bodyguard*?"

I laugh and link my arm with hers. "God no, he's someone else's bodyguard – he's tailing me to make sure I don't attack his boss or whatever."

She throws back her head and laughs. "Girl, your life is *crazy*."

She's the only person here that knows a thing about my real life.

"But seriously, he's looking at you like you're about to be a snack."

I giggle. She's probably not wrong.

"Hey, K." One of the guys appraises my outfit with his eyes as he greets me – he's a wicked hip hop dancer, talented as shit – so I put up with his constant ogling.

"What's up, Robbo?"

"You out there tonight, girl?"

I snort a laugh. "Am I ever not?"

His gaze catches on something over my shoulder and he frowns.

I glance to where he's looking and see Jared, just standing there, openly staring at me.

"Hulk has got the hots for you, girl." Court swoons.

"Ignore him; pretend he's not even there." I tug her arm so she's facing away from my new shadow.

"No can do, K." She twists around again and tries to wave to him.

I bat her hand away. "Down, girl."

"We good, K?" Robbo asks stiffly, still eyeing Jared cautiously.

"It's fine. He's with me, we're good – just ignore him, honestly."

Robbo looks less than convinced, but he doesn't push me on it.

"Where is everyone?"

Wolf – one of the other guys – whistles loud and hollers, "Team talk, yo."

The crew gathers around, all waiting to see what we're going to do tonight.

We'll dance – this isn't a battle, there's no turf war, no struggle for power or anything like that stuff you see in the movies.

Out here it's just a bunch of dancers that want to show their shit – do their thing.

Most people in these circles have nothing, or close to it, but they *do* have dance. That three-and-a-half minutes between the start of a track and the end of it is their happy place.

That's not to say that there's no danger here – shit has been known to go down – but for the most part nothing goes further than the dance floor... whatever random street that dance floor might be located on.

"Listen up!" Wolf booms as we all huddle up.

The chatter dies down and everyone looks to me.

I'm not officially the leader of our little group, but everyone always seems to look to me for guidance.

"You guys ready to do what we've been practising?"

Their heads all nod in unison, excited grins spreading across their faces.

"Hell yes," Court whoops.

We get together and practise about three times a week in a park down town, or at the community hall... never anywhere like the fancy studios I pay a fortune to dance in.

This is the first time we'll perform the new routine to anyone but us.

"You think we've got this, K?" Ava, one of the younger girls asks me nervously.

I wink at her. "Hell fucking yes we do."

CHAPTER ELEVEN

Mack

Well *shit*.

Here I was thinking that a lap dance was sexy.

That had *nothing* on this. When I followed her tonight, I had no idea what I was getting myself into, but *damn* am I glad I came.

This is straight out of one of those chick flick dancing movies, I swear to god. I didn't know this kind of thing went down in the real world.

There's a circle of people surrounding her and her friends as they dance, and I got myself front and centre for this little performance.

Kinsley is right in the middle, looking every inch the sexy siren as she twists and turns her hips to the pulsating beat.

I don't know if she's the boss here or what – I wouldn't be surprised – but the others seem to gravitate towards her, as though she's the main attraction and they're only there to make her look good.

Maybe it's just me that sees it that way, because hell, I can barely pull my eyes from her long enough to really see the others at all.

I don't know what I thought was going to happen in this circle of random people, but *this* was not it.

I know one thing for sure though, Kinsley *is* an incredible dancer. No billionaire control freak father is going to be able to take that away from her.

She catches my eye as she prowls forward to the music.

The beat engulfs the two of us and I see nothing but her.

She smirks, a sexy, smart grin, those pouty damn lips pushed out to perfection, before brushing up against me, her arms wrapping around my neck as she shakes her lithe body.

"*Christ*," I groan.

I want to pick her up and have my way with her right here in front of all these hood rats.

Her eyes dance with mischief as she bites her lip, her hands trailing down to my chest.

She pushes hard, *almost* moving me, and turns on her heel, the crowd cheering as she struts away full of sass.

I chuckle.

This fucking woman.

***

I lean against the grotty concrete wall, my arms crossed firmly across my chest.

She might seem perfectly at ease out here – clearly she's no stranger to these types of hangouts, but I can't seem to convince myself that it's okay to leave her with this rough crowd.

Maybe Gilly's right and I have lost my mind after all.

Kinsley is like gravity – no matter how hard I try to stay away, or how rationally I know that it's a bad idea to go anywhere near her, I can't for the life of me make it happen. She just pulls me right back in.

She glances over her shoulder at me and smirks, before turning back to the girl with the red hair and saying something that makes her laugh.

I've been off the clock for hours – none of this is about work anymore, and while I'm aware I told her I won't touch her while she's still a threat to the boss, I'm pretty confident I'm about to make a liar out of myself.

I don't know how I could resist her after that.

The redheaded chick gives Kinsley a shove in my direction and points her thumbs up at me.

Kinsley's facing me now, stalking towards me, those light blue eyes locked on mine.

"That was some show," I say, my tone gruff as she comes to a stop in front of me.

She pops a shoulder. "Now you know how I dance."

I certainly fucking do.

I glance at the thinning crowd over her shoulder and notice one of the guys she danced with earlier is glaring at the two of us.

I chuckle. "Your boy over there doesn't look too happy about you talking to me."

She follows my line of sight before turning back and rolling her eyes.

"That's just Robbo. I think he was born scowling."

The corner of my mouth twitches. "You sure you don't want to go back over to him?"

She takes a step closer to me, her arm brushing mine. "Oh, I'm sure." She trails a single finger from the neck of my shirt down to my abdomen. "Men have *got* to stop thinking they know what's best for me," she purrs, her tone seductive.

Fuck it all, *I* know what's best for her right now and it involves her on her back, beneath me.

She pouts those god damn sexy lips and tilts her head as she looks up at me as if to say, 'what now?'.

"Screw it," I growl at the same moment that my hands land on her hips and drag her closer.

I bury my face in her neck, her head tipping to the side to give me better access.

She moans, and I forget where I am. I forget everything that isn't her, me and this moment.

She's in my arms and pressed against the wall in a flash, her back hitting with a soft thud. My lips are on her soft skin, kissing and nipping from her ear to the hollow of her throat.

She moans again. "*Jared.*" Her voice is breathy, light and filled with pleasure.

My name has never sounded so good.

"Get a fucking room!" a male voice calls from behind us.

Kinsley giggles, and just like that, the moment is over, I remember where I am again. "I fuckin' hate Robbo," I growl as she slides down my body, her feet hitting the ground.

"That's twice now you've had me up against a wall and failed to come through with the goods, big guy," she teases.

I plant one hand on either side of her head, caging her in. "Who said I was done?"

She leans in close, her lips barely brushing mine as she whispers, "Another time."

She presses her mouth to mine, one soft kiss before she ducks under my arm.

I close my eyes and lean my forehead against the wall in frustration.

I'm in so much trouble here.

I roll my head to the side to see where she went, but she's already disappeared from sight.

I chuckle to myself and jog down the alleyway after her.

Then I tail her the entire way home.

CHAPTER TWELVE

Kinsley

"Darling?" my father calls down the hallway.

I shove the clothes that I wore out the other night under my bed.

I left them hidden in the laundry when I got home that evening and the very next morning they were on the end of my bed, clean and folded neatly in a pile.

Monica knows a hell of a lot about me that she keeps hidden from my father, and I'm grateful for that.

I owe that woman an awful lot.

"In here, Daddy," I call back, cringing at the way my voice sounds as a grown woman calling her father 'daddy.'

He pauses in the doorway and glances down at me, sitting cross-legged on the floor in a full-length evening gown.

"Are you ready?"

"Just need to put on my shoes."

He strides into the room and offers me his hand to get up off the floor.

He's requested another long-sleeve gown, which means we're in the company of business royalty tonight. He always ensures my tattoos are covered when we're going out to something like this.

Heaven forbid I have anything unique about me that someone might notice or think is out of the ordinary.

I still recall the purple shade his face went when he found out I'd got them.

He lets me use his arm for balance as I slip on each of my dainty, fancy little shoes.

"Perfect," he says as he spins me in a slow circle.

He's looking handsome in a black suit and blue tie. His hair is dark like mine and we share the same eyes.

I look nothing like my mother. I'm one hundred percent my father's daughter.

I've often wondered if he'd have such a fondness for me if I happened to have wound up looking like her.

"You look beautiful, my darling," he praises.

I smile. "Thank you, Daddy." I might hate all this showy shit that he makes me go to, but I never grow tired of hearing him tell me that I look nice.

He's the only man I know that isn't trying to get me into bed when he compliments me.

"The car is waiting out front."

"Good, I'm starving."

He chuckles as he leads me out. "Be on your best behaviour tonight, darling."

"Aren't I always?" I smirk to myself.

***

I touch up my already-flawless lipstick again. I've been hiding out here in the bathroom stall for the past fifteen minutes. I've got the toilet lid down so I can sit and everything.

I'm a really classy lady when I want to be.

I snap my compact mirror shut and tuck it into my bag as I hear the main door open.

It sounds like two women entering.

"So much for a super-secret location."

"I know, right? My sister wasn't meant to tell anyone – she'll probably end up getting fired from that catering gig, but she's got *the biggest* mouth."

"Are you and Tim going?" one asks the other.

I slide my lipstick into my bag and sit quietly. You never know what kind of useful information you might hear in a women's bathroom, and quite honestly, I've got nowhere more interesting to be.

"*Of course*, as much as I can't stand the guy, it'll still be the party of the year."

I hear a giggle. "Me too, he's a total asshole, but I can't wait for Saturday."

"It's a shame that Kent won't be there, you two would make *the cutest* couple."

My ears prick up at the mention of my father's name.

"He won't be there?" I hear disappointment in the tone.

Pack it in, sweetheart, I think to myself – I'm not looking for a new step mum.

"Nope." The one with the information smacks her lips together. "He and William *hate* each other."

William...

Oh, now I'm *really* listening.

"That's too bad," the other one replies, and I can almost hear the pout in her voice. She really must think my dad is a bit of alright. She should know better than to be disappointed – if she hangs out with men like William when she knows full well he's a douche, then she's not the right kind of woman for my father.

"I can't believe Liana married him after only knowing him *three* months." One tsks.

"Right? Two years on, still going strong though. Gotta give her credit for putting up with him for this long – god knows I wouldn't have."

They giggle.

"We better go back, Tim will be wondering where I went."

"I better get my flirt on with Mr. Billionaire Barlett *now* then, since he won't be at the anniversary party."

I listen to them giggle and make little comments about how hot my dad is until the bathroom door swings shut again.

I open the toilet door and smirk at myself in the big wall mirror.

Well, well, well... things just got interesting.

CHAPTER THIRTEEN

Mack

"Boss wants to see you, Mack," Gilly tells me as he flops down into a chair on the other side of the room.

"What's it about?"

"If he was willing to tell *me*, he wouldn't need to see *you* now, would he?"

I toss the folder I've been reading through onto the desk and glare at him. "How'd he seem?"

William's moods have been all over the show this past week – I can't decide if getting out of the house has been good for him or not.

Temperamental bastard.

Aside from Kinsley showing up at Liana's yoga class the other day, there's been no sign of her – I don't know how I feel about that either.

She's bat shit crazy, there's no denying that, but hell, I want to get close to her all the same.

"Grumpy – he's starting to spin out about the anniversary party."

I huff out a laugh – we'll lock that thing down tighter than Fort Knox. That party should be the least of his worries. If I were him, I'd be more concerned about what I'd done to piss off Kinsley Barlett than a stuffy party filled with snooty rich people.

"I'll be back," I tell him as I get to my feet, intending to go right up and see the boss now, but apparently Gilly has other ideas.

"You taken that little fruit loop out on a second date or what?"

I stop in my tracks and spin around. "Be kinda hard, seeing as I haven't taken her on a first yet."

He raises his brows at me, a smug grin spreading across his face. "*Yet*." He howls with laughter. "Just admit it, Mack, you've got a thing for the crazy chick."

"I'm not admitting anything."

"You don't even have to; I can see it on your face."

I cross my arms across my chest. "Out of the two of us, which one has had a female steal his dirty underwear?"

"Guilty." Gilly raises a hand, still grinning.

"And who almost got conned into marrying a woman because he'd knocked her up, only to find out she wasn't ever pregnant in the first place?"

"At least it was only *almost*," he grumbles, his smile slipping.

"And which of us—"

"Yeah, yeah," he interrupts. "I get your point."

I smirk.

"Still doesn't change the fact that you're hot for an insane woman."

"She's not insane... she's motivated."

"Motivated to get *what*?"

"If I knew that, I wouldn't need to tail her now, would I?"

I might be here today, but that's not to say I haven't got eyes on her at all times.

"Maybe you're chasing that tail for entirely different reasons." He waggles his brows at me, his grin reappearing.

"Maybe you need to mind your business," I call as I get the hell out of that room.

The last thing I need is Gilly knowing how genuinely close I am to being balls-deep in that particular type of trouble.

I knock once on William's door, but don't wait to be told to come in – he's the one who summoned me here after all, but when I enter, it's not what I expected – he and Liana are sitting side by side on the couch.

I turn and make a beeline for the door again. "Sorry, I'll come back."

"No, we're waiting for you," Liana says quickly, "please sit."

I eye her curiously as I slowly approach them and do as she's requested.

Liana is rarely involved in any of the security procedures, and even though I like her a whole lot more than William, her presence here suggests a problem – one that I'm bound to have to deal with.

"Is something wrong?"

Liana glares at William who looks guilty as hell, before looking my way again.

"William has finally come clean about that... *woman*."

I raise my brows at her in question, as though I have no idea who she's referring to. Last thing I want to do is speak out of turn and put my foot in it – as much fun as it might be to throw the boss under the bus.

"Kinsley Barlett." She says the name with a tinge of distaste. "He's told me that they... *spent the night* in each other's company before we met, and that recently she has *made her presence felt* – shall we say."

That's one way to explain it – she's certainly made her presence felt where I'm concerned.

I can feel a pulse of energy thrumming through my veins right now, just from talking about her.

I nod. "Alright then. Has something happened with Ms. Barlett?"

I'm confident nothing has slipped past my defences. We run a tight ship around here; I screen all the mail and one of us is with Liana or William at all times if they leave this house. Combine that with the electric fence and the drooling dog and I'd say we're covered – Kinsley might be resourceful, but even she's not that good.

"Not since she showed up at Liana's yoga class," William grumbles.

"That situation was handled quickly and efficiently," I tell him. "I've got eyes on her at all times now, so if she tries anything else, we'll be one step ahead."

Liana tips her head and eyes me curiously.

William's phone rings and he glances at the screen. "I have to take this." He gets to his feet and leaves the room, closing the door behind him.

"I heard one of the guys talking about you taking her out for coffee after you left the yoga studio..." Liana prompts me.

She's still watching me closely – too closely for my liking.

"I did." I shrug. "Keep your friends close and your enemies closer..."

"She's a beautiful woman."

"She certainly is," I agree as I sling my arm casually over the back of the couch.

"Do you know what she wants from Will?"

I hear William's voice drawing closer to the closed door and I shake my head. "He's not talking, and neither is she." I lower my voice. "But if I can say one thing, Liana... just between me and you, what William *is* telling me – it's not adding up – there's something we're missing, and I fully intend to get to the bottom of it."

She nods her head to acknowledge she's heard me right as William opens the door again.

It's my phone that sounds now, and I quickly pull it out of my pocket, recognising the ringtone immediately.

"Tom. What is it?"

Tom's tailing Kinsley as we speak, and if he's calling, I doubt it means anything good.

"I've been following her all day, Mack, and there's been nothing to report."

"And now?" I bark, turning sideways to avoid Liana's curious stare.

"Well... now there's *something* to report."

"You gonna spit it out or what? I'm a busy man."

"She's *here*."

"Here, *where*?" I demand.

"The front gate," he replies sheepishly.

I growl and get to my feet, exiting the room without so much as a backwards glance.

I still don't know what the two of them wanted, but we'll have to get to the bottom of it another time – my shift is about to end, and I've got more pressing matters to deal with it would seem.

I stride to the other side of the house and glance out the window.

Sure enough, her black Audi is parked at the gate, Tom's white SUV right behind it.

I watch as the driver's door of the Audi opens and she steps out.

"Jesus Christ, what is she wearing?" I hiss into the phone.

"Fuck-me boots, Mack. God damn fuck-me boots," Tom replies, his tone pained.

I can see why he's having trouble speaking... my dick is hard from just looking at her.

"Shit, she's coming this way, what do I do?" he asks.

I watch as Kinsley approaches his car and taps on the driver's side window.

"See what the hell she wants," I demand.

I hear him press the button and see his window lowering.

"Hi, Tom," I hear her purr, "I'm going to need to speak to Jared, is the big guy available?"

I don't hear him answer, but he must nod his head because she continues.

"That's him on the phone, isn't it?"

"Yes, ma'am."

"Hey, big guy," she says, louder this time so I can be sure to hear her, "I'm going to need you to come out here."

My feet are already moving before she even finishes her sentence.

***

I tip my head at Tom and his window slides shut.

He backs up his SUV and peels off down the street. He'll stay close enough that I can call on him and have him back here within minutes, but not so close that he's going to be listening in on my conversation.

I press a button on my cell phone and the gate slides open, just enough to let me out. I doubt she's going to be running anywhere fast with the size of the heels on those boots, but she's certainly full of surprises.

She's leaning against the driver's side door, watching me.

"This is a new tactic," I drawl. "I guess knocking on the front door is worth a try."

"You gonna let me in, big guy?" She arches a dark brow at me.

I chuckle and cross my arms across my chest. "C'mon now, K, where would the fun be in that?"

She reaches up and runs a hand through the black glossy strands of her hair, the motion causing the hem of her skin-tight black dress to ride up even higher.

She's fucking good, I'll give her that. She'd have had Hughy eating out of the palm of her hand by now.

"I'm fairly confident this isn't a social visit, so how about you tell me what it is you came here for."

"I came to talk to *you*," she replies.

"Talk then, Kinsley, my shift ended ten minutes ago."

Truthfully, there's nowhere I'd rather be than right here talking in circles with this infuriating woman, but she doesn't need to know that.

"I hear you're having a little party."

Shit.

Shit, shit, shit.

"Are we?" I reply, my tone far more relaxed than I really am.

"That's the word on the street," she says with a smirk.

She's like a bloodhound when it comes to sniffing out information about the boss.

I don't know how the hell she heard about it, but I'm not too concerned. None of the guests have been told where the party is being held yet, as far as I'm aware, only William, Liana and my team are aware of the specifics, but Kinsley always seems to know more than she lets on, so I'd be smart not to underestimate her.

"What are you planning, Kinsley?"

I figure I may as well cut right to the point. She came here for something – she's not just planning to reveal her hand and walk away – she wants to make a deal.

"I came to offer a peaceful solution to this little *problem*."

"Go on."

"Option one... you let me in here now, and I talk with William and Liana, I... *we* do this quiet. Civilised."

"And option two?" I frown at her.

I can't think of anything she could say that would make option one the winner, but I'll hear her out.

"Or option two..." she carries on, "I turn up at the party and we have this little chat in front of *all* their family and friends." She smirks at me, a cocky grin.

"There might be a problem with that little plan, fruit loop... you don't know where the party is, and even if you did, you'd have to get past my men – past *me* – and I just don't see that happening."

"But are you sure I don't know where it is?"

My brow furrows.

Her grin deepens. "You spend much time in women's bathrooms, big guy?"

"I can't say I have."

"You should." She nods in encouragement. "It's amazing the secrets you hear."

I narrow my eyes at her. She knows. Or she wants me to think she knows. Only god knows which one of the two it is, or in this woman's case, the devil.

I can't tell if she's playing me or not.

Fuck.

I need to think fast.

I hold up one finger at her, indicating that I want her to wait a minute.

"Go ahead," she says.

There's no way the boss is going to let her in – and I can't even suggest it to him – doing so would give the impression that I have no faith in the security plan I've put in place for the party two nights from now. But I can't do *nothing* either – I need a god damn third option.

I pull my phone from my pocket. Gilly answers on the second ring.

"Those are some sexy fucking boots, Mack," he says by way of hello.

"Gilly," I bark at him, "Can you do me a favour?"

"Depends what it is," he drawls.

"Bring my truck around front," I tell him, my tone hushed now.

"You got a plan?" he questions.

"I've got *something*." I grimace as I hang up the phone.

Kinsley raises her brows at me in question and I prowl towards her, pinning her against her car in a flash, my hips flush against hers.

"You're always causing trouble for me," I growl.

She bites down on that bottom lip of hers, and I swear I almost forget what I'm doing here.

"Your move, big guy," she purrs.

The sound of the gate opening spurs me into action.

I reach through her open window and yank her keys from the seat.

"What are you doing?" she shrieks as I grab her and toss her over my shoulder.

"Going with option three," I growl as I deposit her into the passenger seat of my four-wheel drive.

"Hey, Kinsley." Gilly grins at her from the driver's seat as I buckle her up.

I round the front of the hood and he meets me halfway.

I toss him her keys, and he hands me mine.

"Good luck, Romeo." He chuckles.

I can hear Kinsley yelling and cursing as she desperately tries to get the door open.

"Yeah, thanks, I think I'm going to need it."

CHAPTER FOURTEEN

Kinsley

"They have a name for people like you, you know that, right?"
I glare at him as he pulls into an enclosed garage, the huge door
behind us sliding shut before he's even turned the engine off.

"Let me guess... *'assholes'*?"

"Kidnappers!" I shriek at him.

He chuckles. "C'mon now, fruit loop, don't be mad that I
one-upped you. You played your hand and I played mine... one
of us had to come out on top."

I smirk at him. "If you're going to be on top, at least be doing something that we'll both enjoy."

He shakes his head in amusement as he swings his keyring
around his finger arrogantly, like he hasn't got a care in the
damn world.

I pout. "Where the hell are we?"

"Technically we're nowhere," he says right before I feel the
car shake and start to descend.

My eyes widen. "I swear to god, Jared, if you're taking me
to some kind of kinky underground lair, I'll—"

"You'll *what*?" he asks, his tone cocky as he spreads his legs
further apart.

He's got black jeans on today that hug his ass, and a white
t-shirt stretched tight over his biceps.

He looks like a tasty snack. Actually, correction, a tasty meal. Jared McKenzie could never be a mere snack.

"I'll put it to good use," I reply sassily, a wide grin stretching over my face.

I want to be pissed off, I really do – but I'm excited. I'm really not right in the head.

"There's my girl." He chuckles and the simple sentence makes my stomach flutter.

"Seriously, big guy, where are we?" I try and look out the window, but it's too dark, I can't make out anything.

"You'll see," he murmurs.

The movement stops and sensor lights flick on, one by one, until the entire length of the huge room is illuminated.

"Out you get."

I glance warily at him before opening the car door and stepping out.

We're in a massive garage and, judging by the fact that we just took some type of lift downwards, I assume we're underground. This room is big enough for him to drive his huge vehicle off the lift platform and turn it around if he wanted to. He has a motorbike to the right, and the idea of him riding that thing has me drooling.

"Kinsley." His gruff voice drags my attention back to him.

He's standing with his arm outstretched towards me, his hand open and waiting for me to take.

I shouldn't want to hold hands with a man who just essentially kidnapped me, but I'd only be lying if I said I didn't.

I reach for him and he clasps my hand in his much bigger one.

Everything about him is bigger than me, it's mouth-watering.

"This is my house," he tells me as he leads me through the garage, heading towards a door at the far end.

"You live down here?" I ask in disbelief.

"Sure do."

"Are we going to be trapped if the power goes out?"

He shakes his head. "Generator. But you're trapped here regardless." He smirks and taps a code into the panel near the door.

He doesn't even attempt to hide it from me, and I raise a brow in question. "It changes every hour," he explains.

I'm impressed. I guess security *is* his forte after all.

He opens the door, towing me in behind him.

I can see light up ahead, but it's not like the artificial light in the garage, it's natural light.

I frown in confusion – we're underground...

He indicates with his head for me to go ahead and check it out, so I do; my curiosity has got the better of me.

I wander down the short hallway, and when the room opens up in front of me, I gasp.

It's the ocean.

I turn back to him. "*How?*"

He takes my hand again and leads me out the huge, open glass door and onto the balcony.

"Holy shit," I breathe. *That's* how.

We're *in* the cliff face. His house is built into the cliff.

I glance over the railing and take in the hundred or so metre drop to the crashing ocean below.

"You can't get out of here that way." He smirks at me.

"You don't say..."

I know I'm supposed to be shrieking 'kidnapper' and fighting my way out, but no one in their right mind would be trying to escape this paradise.

I didn't even know places like this existed.

"You are clearly too rich to be working security," I say like an accusation. "Family money?"

He leans back against the railing – completely at ease. Ever since he turned off that car engine, he's been totally relaxed – I guess that means there's no way I'm getting out of here.

"You'd be surprised what a man will pay to keep himself safe."

"Especially for someone so willing to *go the extra mile*," I drawl, raising my brows at him.

"Kidnapping was a new low, I'll admit it, but you didn't give me much choice... crashing an anniversary party... that's some crazy shit, baby."

I do my best to ignore the way it makes me feel when he said the word 'baby'.

"You could have let me into the mansion..." I pout.

"And lose my highest paying client? I don't think so."

"It doesn't look like you need the money," I press.

He shrugs. "I don't. My mother was a very wealthy business woman – ironically enough, my father was her head of security when they first met. They got married, had me and proceeded to spoil me rotten."

That makes me smile.

"Where are they now?"

"Retired on a beach somewhere, and they still have a terrible habit of spending too much money on me."

"Huh," I muse. I never considered that we might have something like that in common.

But where I'm often just an extension of my father's wealth – another thing for him to own – this here doesn't feel like that. I very much doubt Mack was given anything as a means of being controlled.

I doubt there's anyone in the world that could control Jared McKenzie if it wasn't what he wanted.

"But enough about my family's money – the reason I work is because I love it – I'm carrying on my father's legacy and, while *I* might not need the cash, some of the guys on my team do, and I like to make it worth their while. They're the best in the biz."

I smirk at him. "All of them?"

He chuckles. "Alright... maybe not Hugh."

"You called them *your* team?"

He nods. "They're employed by me, and I'm employed by Wellman – plus a few other lower requirement clients that we fit in on the side."

"A business man... I'm impressed..."

He smirks and looks at me, his eyes grazing from my head to my toes, leaving behind a trail of heat on my skin.

"What do we do now?"

"You make yourself comfortable, Kinsley, because we're going to be here a while."

I scowl at him. So that's his plan then... keep me here until the party's over and I'm not as much of a threat. "I could have my father's security get me out of here in about thirty seconds flat, you know that, right?"

He shrugs. "I don't think you want to go anywhere... and even if you did, what are you going to tell them? I wasn't kidding when I said we were nowhere... unless they're going to abseil down that cliff face, they're not going to come for you, baby."

I try to be mad but fail miserably. I'm stuck in the middle of nowhere with a handsome-as-fuck man who keeps calling me baby.

Somebody save me.

Not.

CHAPTER FIFTEEN

Mack

I run my hand through my hair and let out a deep breath.

I did *not* think this through.

Sure, in *theory*, it's not the worst idea in the world... but now that she's here, wearing that skin-tight dress and those god damn over-the-knee boots, I'm not so sure about my genius plan after all.

She's in my bathroom right now doing lord only knows what, and all I can think about is fucking her against the shower door.

I've got about a hundred missed calls from William, and one text from Gilly, which simply said 'you're fucked, bro... voodoo pussy'.

I shake my head at the man I call a best mate, but the way she's looking... hell, maybe he might be onto something after all.

I hit dial on my boss's number and wait for him to pick up the call.

"What the fuck are you doing?" he demands.

"Hello to you too," I drawl.

"Cut the shit, Mack. Where the fuck is she?"

He might be my boss, but he sure as hell is getting on my nerves. Nobody speaks to me like that and gets away with it for long.

"I have her under control."

"*Where*?" he snaps at me. "I want to know exactly where that little bitch is."

I narrow my eyes and fight to keep my voice even. He might not be able to see me right now, but if looks could fucking kill...

I don't know what the hell this debacle is all about, but I know one thing – William is keeping secrets. I'm sure Kinsley is too, but maybe *he's* the one I need to be wary of, more so than the stunning raven-haired woman in my house.

Whatever the situation, Kinsley *isn't* a bitch, and he won't get the chance to speak about her like that again. He only gets the one strike when it comes to her.

My jaw ticks as I contemplate answering him. "I have her at my house with me."

He's silent for a beat. "Are you *fucking* my stalker?"

"Not that it's any of your business, but no. I'm not." *Not yet* anyway.

"This isn't right, Mack."

"She was going to crash the party, boss. It was either let her go and wait for her to strike, let her into your house for a chat with you and your wife, or do what I did, and eliminate the threat. You should be thanking me that I'm doing this on my own time."

"You can't keep her locked up forever. She'll be back."

I don't doubt that, but hopefully when I finally do get to the bottom of this, it won't be in front of a few hundred people.

"She will. Maybe if you wanted to tell me what the deal is with you two, I could work on making the problem go away."

He doesn't reply.

"Let me do my job, Will."

He's quiet still, and just when I'm about to give up and end the call, he speaks. "Has she told you what she wants with me?"

I don't miss the nervous edge to his voice.

"*No*," I answer curtly as my gaze slides to the sexy-as-fuck woman who is now leaning against the doorway, watching me intently.

My brows pinch together as William barks something down the phone.

She waves at me smugly, her chin jutting upwards.

She's barefoot now, and somehow, she looks even more appealing than she did with the boots on.

"I gotta go, boss, I'll call you tomorrow." I hang up on him before he gets another word in. I'm done with his shit for the day, I've gone above and beyond here – selfish motivation aside – and the wanker doesn't even appreciate it.

"Work problems?" She smirks when I toss my phone onto the bench top.

I grunt. "Nothing I can't handle."

She strolls towards me, one hand running over the cool marble. "Same way you're going to *handle* me?" she questions as she approaches.

She's the epitome of gorgeous right now – that silky black hair, those full luscious lips, and quite possibly the most beautiful eyes I've ever seen – and that's all before I even get started on her body.

"You're not the kind of woman who can be *handled*, Kinsley... not even by me."

She eyes me for a beat, her tongue darting out to moisten her lips. She's right in front of me now, close enough for me to reach out and take her if I want to.

"You keeping me here all night, big guy?" she purrs.

I nod, my hand snaking out to cup her face.

She leans into my touch. "Am I meant to be pissed about it?"

"I don't care if you are," I growl.

I wrap my other hand around her tiny waist and tug. She stumbles forward and falls into me, her palms pressing flat against my chest.

"I need to tell my father I won't be home tonight."

Her phone got left behind on the seat of her Audi. She's totally helpless, and I'm a sick man, because I love the fact that she's completely at my mercy.

"You're not a little girl," I rasp, my mouth moving to her ear. "Surely you're allowed out for the night without Daddy's permission?"

She hums deep in her throat and grips the front of my shirt in her hands. "The last thing I want is him coming looking and bringing the cavalry."

"You don't want to be rescued?"

"Not from you, big guy. Not anymore."

She tips her face up and brushes her lips ever so softly against mine. "I need to call Court or Robbo too... tell them I'm not going to make it out tonight."

"Fuck Robbo," I growl, slamming my lips against hers.

Her hand snakes into the back of my hair, tugging hard as she moans into my mouth.

I pull away and drag in a deep breath. This woman is literally going to be the death of me.

I reach for my phone and slide it across the bench to her before my self control evacuates the building entirely. "Make your calls."

***

She's twirling her fucking hair around her finger and giggling into my phone like a teenage girl.

It's sexy as fuck.

I've not let her out of my sight since she hit the green dial icon.

I was fairly confident she wasn't going to call her father and have him swoop in and save her, but I figured it couldn't hurt to make my presence known nonetheless.

I was worried about nothing as it turned out, she didn't even call Kent – instead, she called his head of security and told him – *not* asked him – to cover for her. I don't know what dirt she's got on that poor bastard, but it was awfully fucking clear that she had his balls in a vice – a tight one.

Maybe I should be concerned by the amount of men Kinsley has power over, but I'm too busy being impressed. And turned on... *definitely* turned on.

She's talking to her redheaded friend, Courtney, now – the one from the other night and given the amount of coy glances she's been stealing in my direction, I know they're talking about me.

"I'll be back next week," Kinsley promises.

If I've let you out by then, I think to myself.

She giggles at something her friend says and looks at me again, appraising me from head to toe this time. "That leaves me wide open, Court."

I raise my brows at her in question.

"Love you, bye." She hangs up and tosses my phone back to me.

I catch it in one hand, but don't move from my spot. I'm still waiting for an explanation.

"She told me not to do anything she wouldn't do." She pops a shoulder. "Doesn't leave much off limits."

"I knew I liked her better than Robbo." I smirk.

She laughs and strolls over to my sound system.

"What now then, big guy?"

She fiddles around with a few buttons and an old school R&B song starts playing through the speakers. She smirks over her shoulder at me. "Knew you had a bit of ghetto hidden in there somewhere."

I chuckle and push off the wall.

"Dance with me."

I shake my head. "I don't dance."

She sways her hips and twists her arms up above her head. "C'mon, big guy."

I shake my head again, never once taking my eyes off her.

"I can think of a *hundred* other things I'd rather do with you than dance," I growl.

She smirks and turns the knob to lower the volume. "Liar," she purrs as she seductively strolls towards me. "You can only think of *one*."

One thing is certainly standing out, she's not wrong about that.

"But I've got a hundred different ways of doing it," I answer, my mouth tugging up into a grin.

She reaches me then, and her arms snake up to wrap around my neck. "It's a shame we met how we did, big guy, I actually kinda like you."

I slide my hands down her sides and around to her ass.

She gasps as I hoist her effortlessly into my arms, her legs wrapping around my waist.

"It doesn't matter how we met."

"I think it might... you're holding me hostage in your house."

"Exactly," I breathe. "You think you'd be here if I didn't want you to be? There's a million places that I could have taken you, *should* have taken you, Kinsley... but I *didn't* – I brought you *here* because you're all I can think about." I rest my forehead against hers.

She bites down on her full bottom lip. "I'm glad you did," she whispers.

"I want you so badly I can't think straight."

"Thinking straight is for suckers," she rasps.

I chuckle.

She's not wrong.

"Having you here might benefit William, but don't for a second think that you're here for anybody other than *me*, Kinsley."

She nods. "I believe you."

I claim her mouth with mine, tugging her bottom lip between my teeth. She moans and I push my tongue into her mouth, kissing her with every bit of pent up sexual tension in my body.

She gives back as good as she gets, her hands weaving into my hair as she grinds her hips against mine.

My phone rings loud and shrill in my pocket and I curse under my breath.

"Leave it," she purrs as she kisses me again.

I groan in agreement and the ringing stops.

I take a couple of steps in the direction of the couch and the fucking thing starts up again.

I know it's Gilly, that's his ringtone.

"He's just going to keep on calling until I take it," I murmur against her lips.

"Answer it then." Her voice is breathy and light – like I've stolen the volume right out of it.

I reach the couch and sit down, her in my lap.

I slide my phone from my pocket and hit 'answer'.

"This better be important, Gilly."

"Not in the slightest," he replies, his tone amused.

I swear the dude seriously has a radar that lets him know when it's the most inappropriate time to call me.

Kinsley dips her head and starts kissing my neck, her teeth grazing my skin.

Jesus Christ.

I hold back a groan.

"What do you want, G? I've got my hands full here."

I grab the hem of her dress, which has ridden right up her thighs and pull it up further, exposing her black lace underwear.

I grab hold of her sexy ass and squeeze gently.

She slides her hands under my t-shirt and grazes my abdomen with her fingernails.

There's no avoiding my groan this time.

"Are you wanking off right now?" Gilly demands.

"Not even close." I grind the words out between gritted teeth.

Kinsley's hands work at the button on my jeans, and if I don't get off this call soon, he won't be far off with his accusation.

"You're fucking around with her, aren't you?"

"What do you want, Gilly?" I repeat my question, neither confirming nor denying.

"Please tell me you're not seriously entertaining the idea of letting that crazy bitch near 'little Mack'?"

Kinsley giggles and pauses for a second, clearly having heard what Gilly said.

"Don't name my dick, it's weird, man." I let my head fall back against the back of the couch.

Kinsley takes that as her cue to begin nibbling and sucking on the skin there. I groan again.

"You've lost your mind."

Maybe I have.

"I bet she's a *freak* in the sheets though..."

I'm so fucking hard right now, nothing – not even my best mate hearing, is going to be able to stop me from having my way with her.

"Gilly, I'm only going to ask this once more, what the fuck do you want? Because if you don't get off the phone shortly, you're going to hear a hell of a lot more than a bit of groaning and heavy breathing, you know what I'm saying?"

"I don't want anything... and I'm not against a bit of phone sex." He chuckles.

I hang up.

That bastard will be the death of me one of these days, I swear to god.

"You about done chatting?" she purrs in my ear.

I find the zip on the back of her dress and slide it down, tugging the sleeves until it's bunched around her middle.

Her black lace bra matches her underwear and I get even harder.

I don't know who I thought I was kidding, trying to resist her – we were always going to end up here. I'm just as weak as the men I once made fun of wherever she's involved.

She tugs on the hem of my shirt and I scoot forward so she can pull it over my head.

"You're so fucking sexy."

"*Show me* how sexy."

I growl as my lips get to work. I don't need to be told twice.

CHAPTER SIXTEEN

Kinsley

"Oh my god, Jared, *yes,* I need more," I moan.

He chuckles as he spoons another huge pile of pasta into my bowl. "If those carbs get you off better than I did, my pride is going to be wounded."

I wink at him. "Don't worry, big guy, little Mack got the job done."

He groans and throws his head back, every muscle in his tight and toned torso bunching and flexing. "Fucking Gilly."

"He sounds like a bit of fun."

"He's a handful – you two would probably get on well actually."

"Oh, ha ha." I roll my eyes at him and shove another forkful of pasta into my mouth.

He ordered takeaway for us about a half-hour ago.

This being held hostage thing isn't working out too bad.

So far, I've had the hottest sex of my life, a soak in a huge tub overlooking the ocean, and been fed the best Italian food in town.

I might never leave.

I'm not stupid enough to think that this is about anything more than keeping me out of William's way, with a side of sexual attraction thrown in, but hey, beggars can't be choosers.

That's all men see when they look at me.

I'm not the type you take home to your mum; I'm the one you fuck in a hotel for a one-night stand.

It pains me to think that that was all this was between us – but it's the reality.

I'm not going to stop until I take William down, and Jared isn't going to just roll over and let me do it.

We're going to butt heads at every turn, and while that might be all fun and games here, where we're alone and mostly naked – I know this bliss won't last forever.

Even if I weren't gunning for the man he'd been hired to protect, Jared McKenzie wouldn't be interested in anything more than sex with a woman like me – I'm too much work.

I feel him behind me, he sweeps the hair from my neck and trails soft kisses up to my jaw. "What's got you frowning, baby?"

I like the way he calls me *baby* far too much.

I shouldn't have slept with him – I'm catching the feelings.

It might not happen with every guy I sleep with, but it's happening now, and it's a problem.

I like Jared, I really do. He's the kind of man a girl like me dreams about.

He sees my crazy and runs towards it, not away from it.

I shake my head and plaster on a fake smile. I spin on my stool so I'm facing him, and he plants one of his strong, muscular arms on the bench on either side of me.

He makes me feel so small and delicate.

He makes me feel protected and safe – even though the reality is it's not *me* he's protecting.

He kisses me firmly on the lips. "I like you in my house, Kinsley Barlett."

I want to believe him, I *really* do – but this is nothing more than a game of cat and mouse, and I need to remember that.

"How long am I staying?" I ask, arching a brow in question.

"We'll see," he growls, his eyes smouldering.

He'll be shooing me out the door the minute that party's over, I can already see it coming.

I consider just coming out with it right now – telling him what I want with the Wellman's... but he won't believe me – men never do.

He's on William's team – not mine.

Maybe I should just enjoy the time I have here and forget about the real world for a couple of days.

I lean forward and wrap my arms around his waist.

He's so fucking hot... it should be illegal to look this freakin' good.

I can handle another day of this, I decide.

"Can I ask you something?" he says, his voice curious.

He brushes a strand of hair from my forehead and tucks it behind my ear, and I melt.

"Go for it, big guy."

"You don't have a kid running around somewhere, do you?"

"No..." I furrow my brow. "That was a weird question..."

He frowns to himself before grinning, his features relaxing again. "Just exploring a theory," he replies cryptically.

I can't judge, my head is swirling with theories of my own.

He pushes off the bench and strolls towards the huge television on the far wall.

He hits a button on the wall and a door slides open, revealing hundreds and hundreds of DVDs.

"Holy shit." I gape.

"Horror, action, romance, comedy... what's your guilty pleasure?"

He glances back at me, looking for an answer.

"Action," I reply as I swing my legs down off the stool and pad over to him.

He points to what must be the action section, and I snag 'Aquaman' off the shelf.

I've been dying to see this movie.

He groans. "I can't compete with Jason Mamoa, baby. Can't you pick something with a less attractive main character?"

I pat him on the shoulder. "That's okay, I can just close my eyes and pretend you're him."

"That hurts, you know?" He presses the button and the door slides closed again. "Right down deep in here." He rubs the spot on his chest where his heart is, and I can't help but take a long, slow, appreciative appraisal of his half-naked body, because holy shit it's a sight. He's wearing nothing but his jeans – sans boxer briefs, and they're slung low on his hips, the 'v' that makes smart girls stupid teasing me.

I don't know how often he works out to stay in that kind of shape, but *damn*... it's worth it.

He chuckles smugly, having seen my little eye fuck, and strolls across the room, hitting another button that has a blind descending over the window, blackening the room.

I follow and flop down on the couch.

He holds his hand out for the DVD as he doubles back towards the player.

"You really want to watch a movie with me?" I ask as I pass it to him.

He frowns at me. "Why wouldn't I?"

"Don't you just want to go back to the bedroom and fuck me again?" I ask, and I'm stupid because I actually care about his answer.

He eyes me curiously. "Why do I feel like that's a trick question?"

I shrug, and he crouches down in front of me, bringing us eye level with one another.

"Kinsley?"

"Men only ever want one thing when it comes to me," I whisper.

He reaches out and cups my face tenderly with his big hand.

"Well I want more than just one thing."

"You *do*?" I hate the vulnerability in my voice. I usually hide it, bury it deep and cover it with sass and attitude, but he stripped that back the minute he looked at me the way he is right now.

"I don't think you understand what you do to me, baby, and I don't just mean physically." He brushes his rough thumb across my bottom lip. "I'm risking my job, my entire *career* right now with you... it's not something I take lightly, but you're like an addictive habit I can't shake. You might be playing me for all I know, but hell if I care, it'd be worth it for a few more hours with you."

"Jared..." I whisper, my heart thumping rapidly against my ribcage.

I'm not playing with him – not anymore.

"Sexy as sin," he growls. "Crazy as hell... you're a mind-fuck, *Kinsley*, that's what you are, and I've never wanted to figure something out so badly."

His words speak to my messed-up soul, and I lean forward and kiss him, softly at first and then passionately, like I can't get enough, because truthfully, I *can't*.

"Are you pretending I'm 'Aquaman' right now?" he murmurs against my lips.

"You'll never know." I giggle.

He kisses me again, and I sigh.

Who needs Aquaman when you've got Jared McKenzie?

CHAPTER SEVENTEEN

Mack

I stick my head back around the frame of my door and take in her sleeping form again.

She's still out like a light.

The woman is a whole lot of fucked up wrapped in perfect packaging.

I might not know the first thing about her when it really comes down to it, but I do know one thing – men have hurt her – *used* her, and the thought of another man's hands on her body, let alone ones that are using her for nothing but sex, causes my blood to boil.

I don't even know why I care so much – I guess she's not the only one with issues.

I glance at my watch again; it's after ten in the morning.

I know I kept her up late and all, but this is ridiculous. I'm bored.

I hit the button on the wall next to the door and the black-out blind on my bedroom window begins to lift, revealing a strip of dark blue sea.

I stop and leave it only partially up – I might want to wake her, but I'm not an animal.

I stroll out to the kitchen, hitting play on the sound system as I go past on my way to the coffee machine.

If anything is going to get her to wake, it's bound to be the smell of coffee.

I've got no idea if she always takes her coffee black, so I just make mine and try to waft the smell towards the bedroom.

I glance at my watch again as I watch a storm roll in from the sea.

It's a rough day out there today, not that it matters, I've got nothing to do other than be with her.

I hear her feet padding softly across the living room and I grin. Coffee for the win.

I turn to look at her and my breath gets caught in my throat.

She's thrown on one of my t-shirts, and she looks sexy as hell.

In that very moment I seriously consider tossing in my job and keeping her hostage here forever – I've never felt so all-consumed by a woman, and I've tried out my fair share.

"Morning, big guy." She smiles sleepily at me. I've never seen a woman more beautiful.

She's got makeup smeared under her eyes, and her hair is sticking up at every angle, but holy shit, she's stunning.

I can't even speak.

She walks right up to me, wraps her arms around my middle and hugs me tight. I breathe in deeply, inhaling the smell I can only describe as Kinsley.

"Coffee?" I offer.

She smiles and reaches for the cup in my hand.

"I didn't know how you liked it," I explain.

She sips from mine and sighs in satisfaction. "It's coffee, big guy, I'd take it intravenously if I had to."

I chuckle when she offers the cup back to me, her other arm still wrapped tightly around my middle.

"It's all yours, baby."

Her eyes sparkle in appreciation.

I push some of her unruly hair back from her face, my other hand roaming over her ass and up to settle on her lower back.

"You always sleep in so late?"

She shakes her head as she takes another sip of coffee. "*Never*. This was a treat."

Well shit, I feel bad for waking her now.

I kiss her forehead, and her eyes float closed, a dreamy expression on her face.

I point to a stool at the breakfast bar. "Sit. I'll make you breakfast."

She strolls over to the seat I pointed out, her cup clasped between her hands as she hoists herself up. "You know... I think you accidently Googled 'pamper' instead of 'kidnap.'"

"My phone does have a terrible autocorrect feature," I drawl.

Her light giggle floats through my kitchen and punches me right in the gut. I like the sound of it far too much than can possibly be good for me.

"Are you any good at cooking or what?" she eyes me curiously.

"I'm exceptional."

I place a bowl on the bench in front of her, and one on my side of the bench for me, and then grab the box of cereal from the cupboard.

I snag the bottle of milk from the fridge and nudge it her way. "Ta-da."

She raises a brow at me. "You forgot a spoon." The corner of her mouth twitches, a grin playing on her plump lips.

I reach into the drawer and pass her a spoon without taking my eyes from her.

I don't move around to sit next to her – I'd prefer to stay right where I am with a perfect view of her expressions.

She licks her lips.

Fuck it, who needs food? I could quite happily have *her* for breakfast.

"Am I sensing some sexual tension in the air, big guy?"

I realise I'm staring, *hard*. I can't even answer.

She pours herself some cereal, ignores the milk, and dips her spoon into the bowl.

I watch her mouth move as she crunches it.

"You're an excellent chef," she teases.

Jesus. I'm in trouble.

She's seducing me without even trying.

"No milk?" I question as I will my hands to begin working again and make myself some breakfast.

She scrunches up her nose is disgust. "Don't be gross."

I smirk as I reach for the milk and pour it all over my cereal.

"Is this when the torture begins?" She shudders.

I chuckle. She's a funny woman... *sweet*, in a bat shit crazy kind of way.

"So, big guy, what's on the agenda for the day? Assuming you haven't had a change of heart and are willing to let me go?"

I shake my head. There's no way, and it's got less to do with the Wellman's, my job, or my reputation, and a hell of a lot more to do with the way I'm feeling about her.

"I might never give you back," I growl.

Gilly is going to have a field day with this, but when I glance into her crystal blue eyes, I suddenly give a hell of a lot less fucks about what anyone thinks.

"Sure you will." She nibbles on her bottom lip. "I'm a lot of work."

"I've never been afraid of hard work," I say around another mouthful of cereal.

She swirls her spoon around her bowl. "You have no idea what's required to keep a woman like me."

I drop my spoon into the bowl with a clatter.

Truth is, I'm pretty sure I know exactly what's required, my mother, god love her, is wild – she's passionate about a lot of things – and being high maintenance is right there at the top of the list.

I lean across the bench towards her, my arms bracing me. "You're just looking for someone you can trust, you don't fool me, fruit loop."

She tugs the corner of her lip into her mouth and looks at me with wide eyes.

"You're just looking for someone to protect, you don't fool me, big guy." She whispers my sentiments back to me.

She's dead fucking right. And it's not just *someone* I want to protect – it's her.

I lean in a little closer.

"Quit looking at me like that," she breathes.

"Looking at you like *what*?"

"Like I'm the answer to all your problems."

I chuckle darkly. She's the opposite of the answer to my problems – in fact she's a big part of the cause, but that doesn't deter the hunger I know she'll see in my eyes, or the fear blossoming in my chest at the prospect of having to give her up in another twenty-four hours.

Strangely, I feel more complete when she's around, less lonely – so maybe she's right – maybe she *is* the answer after all.

There's nothing wrong with my life without her, but I'm all about improvement.

I can't help but see that Kinsley *would* be an improvement.

"What are you doing to me?" I breathe as she leans across, closing the distance between us and resting her forehead against mine.

"Same thing you're doing to me?" she offers with a shrug.

I can't take it any longer, this distance between us. I round the bench and she turns slowly on her stool, moving with me.

I stop right in front of her, and her knees fall open to welcome me. I nudge them wider and settle between them.

I groan when I glance down and see my shirt has ridden up her thighs and she's bare beneath.

She slides her elbows onto the bench behind her and leans back.

My shirt is clinging to her breasts, her nipples hardening under my stare.

Slowly, I grab the hem of the fabric covering her body and ease it upwards until she's completely exposed to me.

"*Jesus,* Kinsley," I groan as my eyes rake over everything from her head to her toes. "You're so beautiful."

"I feel beautiful when *you* look at me," she whispers, and I can't explain why, but it hurts to hear her say that.

She leans forward and drapes her arms around my bare shoulders. "It feels like more than just sex when I'm with you," she admits, and that vulnerability she gave me a glimpse into yesterday is back – this is the real Kinsley, this woman in front of me now.

And as much as I enjoy the sexy, sassy banter between us, I want this piece of her too.

I want every piece of her.

"That's because it's not just sex... not with you."

She pushes forward, her mouth moulding to mine at the same moment her hand drops to my side.

She drags her nails over my bare skin, and I shudder – it feels so good.

She goes further south until she's gripping me through my boxer briefs.

My hands are everywhere, touching every inch of silky skin available to me.

I drop my head to her breast, and she sighs in pleasure. "*Jared.*"

She slides my boxers down my legs, and this time when I push deep inside her, something changes between us.

CHAPTER EIGHTEEN

Kinsley

"I've got an idea."

I snag the deck of cards off the coffee table and start shuffling them in my hands.

He raises a brow at me before tugging me back into the crook of his arm.

I can't deny how much I like being here – in his arms... in his home...

He kisses the top of my head. "You play?"

I shake my head. "Not really." I wiggle in his arms so I can glance up at his handsome face. "But I've got a game for you."

"I'm intrigued."

My eyes trail of their own accord down his chest and over the sexy tattoo that runs down his bicep.

He chuckles. "You're drooling, baby."

I make a show of wiping my chin. "You might need to put a shirt on so I can focus."

His laugh deepens as he gestures to the shirt I'm wearing of his. "Then you'd have to give that back, and trust me, if you take that off... there's only one thing I'll be focusing on, and I can tell you right now, it won't be a card game."

I feel my cheeks heat. I don't know what it is about this man that turns me soft, but I kind of like it – I can relax a little bit with him, I don't have to act like I'm bullet proof all the time.

I shrug off his arm and shuffle backwards away from him. I cross my legs and split the deck of cards in half.

I hand him half and I keep the other half.

"Low card, high card," I tell him.

He glances at the pile in his hand. "What does a high card get me?"

I smirk. "A question."

His eyes sparkle and the corner of his mouth twitches. "*Any* question?"

"Anything." I confirm with a nod, but then backtrack. "Anything that doesn't involve William Wellman."

He adjusts his big body so it's facing my direction. "Bring it on, baby."

I pop a shoulder. "Flip it, big guy."

I flip a six – he has a ten.

I pout and he raises a fist in the air triumphantly.

"I think I'm going to like this game."

I roll my eyes. "What's the damage?"

"Have you fucked Robbo?"

My jaw goes lax for a fraction of a second before I regain composure.

"You can ask me anything in the world, and *that's* what you're going with?"

He stares pointedly at me, waiting for his answer.

"No," I reply. "I haven't."

"Good," he growls.

"Careful, big guy, you're sounding a little jealous..."

He shrugs. "Better get yourself a high card and you can ask if I am or not."

"Flip," I say, eager for a turn at questioning him.

I get a nine and he flips a king.

He chuckles. "My turn again, baby."

"Motherfucker..." I mutter under my breath. I never should have played games with a man like this.

I twirl a strand of hair around my finger as I wait for him to ask his question.

"Why do you let your father run your life?"

My hair falls from my hand as I glance back up at his face.

That's not a question I was expecting. "I'm not really sure... a mix of fear, gratitude and obligation I guess."

He reaches out and laces his fingers with mine.

"I'm all the family he has, and I don't want to let him down."

"Don't you want your own life? To be you... to dance?"

"That's more than one question," I whisper.

He squeezes my hand. "Humour me."

I shrug my shoulders. "I mean yeah... I want that... I guess I just don't know how to get it."

"You just reach out and take it." His voice comes out gruff, and his eyes see right past my bullshit.

I could do it if I had *him*. I can see that – naive as I'm allowing myself to be – if I had Jared at my side, I could do anything I wanted with my life.

I can't escape his intense gaze. He's seeing me, right down deep inside of me, and I'm not sure I'm ready for that.

"Flip," I say, and my voice is barely audible, but he hears. He drops my hand from his.

He flips his card and breaks eye contact to check who won this round.

I've got a queen and he's got a two.

"I win." I smirk.

"Hit me with it."

"Why did you bring me to your home? You said there were other places you should have taken me instead..."

He's silent for a few beats. "You remember that first day I was waiting for you when you scaled the fence?"

I nod. I'd seen him just once before that, and only from a distance – he was barking orders to his men.

"You weren't affected by me in the least... not like the other guy – I was so pissed, I knew there was no way I was getting past you."

He chuckles. "I'd watched your security tapes over and over again. I already had those sexy legs and full lips committed completely to memory, but I had to see you in person... so I volunteered to keep watch that day – knowing you were due to make an appearance."

He *wanted* to see me?

"You didn't disappoint." He laughs again. "I'd never met a woman so sexy yet so *infuriating*. You got under my skin, Kinsley, long before I laid a finger on you – and you haven't left. That's why I bought you here, because I couldn't bear the thought of taking you anywhere else. I want you *here*."

"But I'm the crazy girl – you said so yourself."

"I guess I like crazy."

I swallow deeply, my throat suddenly dry. He doesn't say anything else, just watches me process everything he's just said.

"Flip," he says after a few beats.

I flip an eight and he gets a four.

"What happens after tonight?" I blurt out the question I've been dying to know the answer to.

I don't want this to be over.

I don't want to lose him.

He flips his card around and around between his fingers as he studies me. "That all depends on you, Kinsley."

"On *me*?"

He nods slowly. "I want you. I don't want this to end – but I have to be able to trust you... and I can't while you're gunning for William."

I know exactly what he's saying. I have to make a choice... William or him.

I need to finish what William started, I *have* to, but the idea of never being like this with Jared again kills me.

We've only just started. I don't want to end it now.

"What's it gonna be, baby?" he presses.

My mind flicks back and forth between my morals... what's right... what's wrong... what I want...

It always comes back to one thing.

Jared McKenzie.

I think about how it felt to have his eyes on me when I danced in the street, how he can set my body alight with the simplest of touches... the way my heart thumps in my chest when he calls me baby...

I can't give him up, and what's more, I don't *want* to.

"I want *you*," I whisper.

"More than you want revenge or whatever you've being trying to get over William?"

"More than I want anything," I reply, my voice strong and sure.

His serious expression morphs into a grin and he lunges for me, his cards flying everywhere.

"Jared!" I shriek as he pushes me back into the plush couch.

"You mean that?" he growls against my lips.

"I mean it," I breathe.

I've barely got the words out before his mouth is on mine, hot, firm and demanding.

"*William* who?" I gasp as his mouth moves lower.

He chuckles. "That's my girl."

I hear the shrill ring of his cell phone, but he doesn't even pause.

"Do you need to get that?" I moan as his hands roam under the shirt of his I'm wearing.

"Get what?"

"Your... phone... is... ringing," I pant.

He chuckles, his unshaven face rubbing against my stomach.

He pushes up with his strong arms, pinning me with his stare as he strides towards his cell. "Don't you dare move."

CHAPTER NINETEEN

Mack

"Gilly, I swear to fucking god, if you've got my house bugged so you can call me when you know I'm in the middle of something, I will hunt you down and kill you."

"If I had the skills to bug your house without you knowing about it, do you really think I'd still be working for your grumpy ass?"

Valid point.

I glance back into the living room and find Kinsley still right where I left her.

"Make it quick, I wasn't kidding when I said I was in the middle of something."

"I don't think I've ever been more concerned for your sanity whilst simultaneously being jealous of your dick," he muses.

I rub my temple. "You've got some serious issues."

"That I do," he agrees. "Anyway, more pressing problems, boss – Hugh and Tom are out. They've got some kind of bug."

"What do you mean they're out?" I demand, my pulse skyrocketing. "Like a stomach bug?"

The fucking anniversary party is tonight, if the two of them aren't around then it only leaves Gilly and Jack from my team – which isn't enough. Even if I bring in a couple of extra contractors, I'll still feel underprepared.

"From what I can gather, it's all go from both ends, Mack."

I grimace. "That was a visual I didn't need."

"You asked." He chuckles. "Those bastards better not have me spewing and pooing – I've got a delicate stomach."

"Yeah, you're really fragile," I drawl.

"So that brings it down to me and Jack."

"Which isn't good enough." I groan.

"I resent that, you know?" he replies, his tone full of mock outrage.

"Shut up, Gilly, I'm trying to think."

"You're going to have to come in, boss. There's no way around it."

I close my eyes in frustration. "I *can't*."

"This chick you're shacking up with isn't the only one out to get the boss, you know? I think you've forgotten that."

I run my hand through my hair in frustration.

He's right. Kinsley isn't the only one who has had problems with the man who employs me – I've been so wrapped up in her that I've been neglecting to keep my mind on the job the way I should be.

I glance at her again and she's watching me pace the room back and forth.

She told me, no more than a few short minutes ago that she wanted *me* – not William, and I guess that this is as good of a time as any for her to put her money where her mouth is.

"Call John," I tell Gilly. "Tell him I want half a dozen more guys."

"Got it," he replies. "And?"

"And I'll be there in a couple of hours," I say, my tone resigned.

Kinsley's brows rise in question, and I look right into her light blue eyes, willing her not to fuck this up.

I care for this woman far more than I should, given how long I've known her – it's going to kill me if she can't keep her word.

I turn away from her.

"What are you going to do with her?" Gilly questions me.

"Let her go, I guess."

"Good call, boss, you know they say if you love something, you should set it free and if it—"

"Shut up," I interrupt him and his shit talk.

He howls with laughter. "I'll see you in a few, Mack."

The line goes dead.

I grind my teeth together in irritation as I place my phone down next to me.

This isn't what I needed right now. Kinsley may have said she chose me, but that was when she was locked away here – away from the world and its temptations.

She had a plan for this party. I know that was before *this*, whatever this is, but I'm still not one hundred percent convinced.

"There's some serious thinking going on in that head of yours," she says, and I turn back around to face her.

"I have to go into work tonight," I mutter.

She nods in understanding. "That explains the look on your face then."

I stand stock still, contemplating my options.

"Come here." She pats the spot next to her on the couch.

I can't seem to move.

She sighs, gets to her feet and walks across the room until we're toe to toe.

She slides her arms around my middle and tilts her head up to look at my face.

"What's wrong, big guy?" she whispers.

"I don't know what to do," I admit.

"Go to work."

"But what about you?"

"I think I can manage without you for a few hours."

"I can't just lock you up and go."

She shrugs her shoulders, and I shake my head again. "If I leave, you leave."

She nods her head in understanding. "And you're worried that I'm going to crash the party."

"I'd be lying if I said it hadn't crossed my mind."

She presses up onto her tip toes and brushes her lips against mine softly. "Go. I'll go home and you can call me when you're done... bring me right back here afterwards."

My hands find her hips and grip tight. "You want to come back?"

She smirks. "You're cutting into my hostage time here, big guy; you're going to owe me."

I drop my forehead to rest against hers, the war in my head still in full swing.

"Alright," I agree with a resigned sigh. "But I'm warning you, baby, when you step out that door, you're still mine... you understand?"

She doesn't answer, not with words anyway.

***

I drop her home and watch as she turns and waves at me before closing the door behind her.

Jesus. Watching a woman walk away shouldn't feel so wrong.

Her black Audi is here somewhere inside the sprawling property that is home to Kent Barlett. I don't quite know how Gilly got in here to return it – charmed his way no doubt, but I've been assured it's here.

I shake off the feeling of dread I've been sporting ever since we left my place and start the engine again.

I pull out of the covered area and back into the pouring rain.

I hit dial on Gilly's number and my car phone syncs, the loud ring echoing through the small space.

"Hey, Mack," he answers as the huge brass gates open to let me out.

"How's everything at the venue?"

"Running smoothly so far – I've got the guys in place – guests are set to arrive in an hour."

"Good," I say with a nod he can't see.

"You drop her home yet?"

"Just now," I reply, my tone clipped. I'm not in the mood to listen to him giving me shit about her.

"You think she's going to try anything?" he asks instead.

"She said she wouldn't."

"You believe her?"

My jaw ticks. "I'm not sure. I want to, but I'm not sure I do."

"Alright," he drawls. "What's your ETA?"

"Give me fifteen. I've got my monkey suit in the back."

"See you then," he says by way of goodbye.

I glance out my window again at the rain pelting my windscreen.

I don't know what the hell tonight is going to bring, but I've got a bad feeling about it.

CHAPTER TWENTY

Kinsley

"Is that you, darling?" my father calls from his study as I attempt to sneak past and into my bedroom.

I push the door open. "Hey, Daddy."

"You didn't come home last night."

"I was out with some friends."

He takes a sip from his crystal glass – scotch, neat, if I had to guess.

"Was that one of your *friends* who brought your car back to the house? Or a friend who dropped you home just now?"

I pop a shoulder. "They're security, rest assured I was well protected and looked after the entire night."

Not a complete lie.

I certainly was well looked after.

I let my thoughts wander to the feeling of Jared's lips on my skin, his hands in my hair... the way it felt to have his big strong body wrapped around mine... the ease in which he can hold me up in his arms...

I was very, *very* well protected.

"Kinsley." My father's voice shakes me back to the present.

"Sorry, I was day dreaming... what did you say?"

"I said, it was lucky you weren't here, we had an unexpected visitor."

I lean against the door frame and wait for him to speak again.

"Your mother," he says, and it's lucky he didn't offer me a drink, because I think the expensive crystal would have just dropped to the ground.

"What the fuck?" I gape.

He sips his drink and nods in agreement.

"She came *here*?" I demand.

"Buzzed at the front gate."

Jesus, the woman must have balls the size of coconuts. Maybe that's where I get my unruly behaviour from.

"What the hell did she want?"

"Money."

I huff out a humourless laugh. "*Money*. The woman is just a walking cliché, isn't she?"

"Unfortunately, she is."

"I hope you didn't give her a dime."

He tips his head to the side and shoots me a sheepish look.

"Daddy, you didn't?"

"Darling, she threatened to make trouble for you."

I laugh again, only this time it's *with* humour, because this is truly ridiculous.

"I can handle myself."

The look he gives me lets me know he doesn't agree with my assessment, but he doesn't say anything.

I don't care if he believes me or not.

He doesn't know the half of what I handle on a daily basis, and I'm not about to blow my cover by telling him about it.

"She'll be back, you realise that, right? You gave her what she wants, and she'll be back for more like the vulture she is."

"I had her sign an agreement. She comes back and I'll have grounds to have her arrested."

I whistle long and low. "That must have cost you a small fortune."

"It was worth it, to see the back of her again... even if it is only for another fifteen years."

He swigs back the last of his amber liquid and reaches for the bottle to pour himself another.

He's struggling with her sudden reappearance – that much is obvious.

"How'd she look?" I ask, my eyes narrowing as he pours a glass far too large for this time of the evening.

"Like shit." He chuckles darkly, and the corners of my mouth turn up in pleasure.

"You ever miss her?"

He lifts his head to meet my stare, his eyes look sad. "All the time."

Those three words threaten to break my heart.

My dad might be a lot of things, but he's a good man when it comes down to it.

"I think about it sometimes... what life might be like if she hadn't have betrayed you, or if her dirty little secret hadn't come forward and told you what happened."

He sits his glass down on his solid-oak desk. "As much as I try to avoid thinking about that part of my life, I'm glad I found out – I can't imagine living a lie and not even knowing I was."

I smile, small and sad. "Thank you for getting rid of her for me, I'm sorry it cost you a bomb."

"You think I did the right thing? I thought you might have wanted to see her..."

I cross the room and kiss his forehead. "Not even a little bit. She's not my parent – you are."

My father might drive me insane, but I know everything he does isn't to hurt me.

He reaches for my hand and gives it a gentle squeeze. I hate seeing the heartache in his eyes.

He should be happy. He should have someone to share his life with other than me.

"Thank you, darling."

"I'm going up to my room," I tell him as I cross the room again.

It's not totally a lie, I am going to my room, but I don't plan to be in there long.

Seeing that pain and hurt in my father's eyes made one thing clear to me – I'm going to that party tonight, and I'm going to make things right.

I just hope that Jared will forgive me for what I'm planning to do.

CHAPTER TWENTY-ONE

Mack

I catch Gilly's eye and tip my head to the side, indicating for him to meet me outside the main room for a debrief.

He gives the huge venue and the guests inside it a quick sweep with his eyes and starts to move towards the door.

"It's too quiet," I tell him once we're out of sight of the guests, my tone hushed.

He shoves my shoulder. "You say that like it's a bad thing. Why are you always waiting for shit to hit the fan?"

"Experience, intuition, life lessons," I offer.

He shakes his head, a relaxed grin on his face. "Chill, Mack, it looks like you tamed the beast. This thing has been in full swing for two hours already and there's been no sight of crazy pants, or anyone else for that matter."

"Just keep your eyes open; I've got a bad feeling."

"You've *always* got a bad feeling."

"And then usually something fucking bad happens, doesn't it?"

"No comment," he replies, because he knows I'm right on the god damn money.

My gut feeling is good – I've learnt I should trust it.

That's why I'm so on edge – if something doesn't go down here tonight then I'll eat my hat.

He throws his arms up in resignation. "Where's this trouble then, huh? Because I'm not seeing it..."

"Mack, you there?" Jack's voice comes through our earpieces.

I shove Gilly. "You had to go and tempt fate, didn't you?"

He shakes his head in exasperation. "You're not happy when it's quiet, and you're not happy when there's drama. There's no pleasing you."

I ignore the man-child in front of me.

"Copy, Jack, what is it?"

"There's a commotion at the west entrance."

I'm already moving, Gilly falling into step beside me.

"What kind of commotion?" I speak into my wrist mic, tugging at my sleeve as I do.

I know we wear the suits to blend in at events like this, but I don't know who the fuck we think we're fooling. It's as plain as the nose on my face that I'm not part of this crowd.

Sure, I might have more money than I know what to do with, but I'm still not willing to throw it around like a tosser.

"There's a couple of drunk guys fighting," he replies.

"Guests?"

"If the monkey suit's they're wearing is anything to go by, I'd say yeah, they're guests."

"Be there in two," I bark.

Gilly rubs his hands together eagerly. "Nothing I love more than roughing up a couple of rich dudes."

I have to laugh at that.

We cross the hall and go through the door that leads to the west entrance.

We find the two men scuffling around, both too drunk to be doing any real damage at all to the other.

Gilly grabs one and Jack, who was doing his best to keep them apart on his own, holds onto the other one.

"She was looking at *me*," the grey-haired one slurs to the one with the black hair.

"As if... old man," the other one drawls.

"Dying your hair doesn't make you young." The grey-haired one wobbles as he points a finger at the other man.

Gilly chuckles. "You're right about that, boss." He claps the shoulder of the man he's restraining – the one with grey hair. "And unless he's dying it downstairs too, the carpets won't match the drapes anyway – chicks notice that shit."

Fuck's sake.

The man gives Gilly a sly smile over his shoulder, and the guy with the dark hair scowls and tries to fight against Jack's hold.

"Gentlemen," I announce loudly, "You're drunk – go home."

"But where's the pretty girl?"

"Yeah... what did you do with the pretty girl?" the grey-haired guy demands.

I glance at Jack, and he shrugs. "When I got here, it was just these two shoving each other."

I shake my head. A couple of grown-ass men acting like children.

"C'mon, boss, let's get you a cab." Gilly starts walking his guy to the door.

"That's where she came from," he mutters. "Maybe there's more out there."

"Mmm maybe," Gilly humours him.

"*What*?" I demand. "You let a woman in from outside?"

"Can't smoke inside," the one Jack is shoving towards the door pipes up.

I grab his shoulder and halt them. "You jackasses let a woman in here?"

"*Relax*," he slurs. "She was just out for a smoke too. She was just eye candy."

"What did she look like?"

He grins. "*Hot.*"

"Anything more specific?" I grind out the words.

"Dark hair... or was it light..."

I give Gilly a look. This isn't good. None of this is good news.

"Chill, Mack, they're drunk, they probably don't even know what they're talking about."

"Get them outside," I order, and my men comply, opening the door and shoving the two wasted guests outside.

"My wife isn't going to be happy," one says to the other.

"Mine either," he agrees wistfully.

"*Unbelievable*," I mutter as I check for myself that the door is locked.

"I want a full sweep," I demand.

"C'mon, boss," Gilly whines. "You heard the guys; some chick just went out for a smoke with them."

"Those two barely know which way is up." I glance at the two men who are making themselves comfortable on the hard ground. They probably decided to wait for their wives.

"You're overreacting."

"Am I?" I ask him, my mind flicking to Kinsley. "You don't think she's capable of it?"

In my mind, I've already decided that she's here. I'd like to be wrong, I really would, but I don't think I am.

I've got a radar when it comes to that woman, and right now it's beeping like crazy.

"Call her," Gilly suggests, his mind working in sync with mine and realising that she's *more* than capable of sneaking in here.

I slide my phone out of my pocket and hit dial on the contact she created in my phone this morning.

It rings.

And rings.

And rings.

"C'mon, baby," I whisper as I turn my back on the guys.

Her voicemail cuts in, "Leave me a message."

"Fuck." I hang up and spin around. "Have the hire guys spread out around the exits – the three of us are doing a sweep."

They're already in motion alongside me.

"What are we looking for, Mack?"

I almost give him a description of the woman who shared my bed last night but decide against it – innocent until proven guilty and all that.

"You'll know when you see it," I reply gruffly.

I point left. "Jack, you go that way – check *every* room."

He immediately sets off.

"Gilly, you've got the right."

He nods.

I'll take the main room. It's crawling with people – if Kinsley really is here, I'll have the best chance of spotting her in amongst that madness.

I bound up the stairs that lead only to a small mezzanine level and rush to the edge of it.

My gaze scans the room, lingering on every woman with dark hair before moving onto the next.

I can't see a hair out of place, but Kinsley should never be underestimated. If she's here – trouble will follow.

I scan the room again, this time looking for William and Liana. They're there in the very centre of the room, surrounded by their friends and family.

I lift my wrist to my mouth. "Jack, anything?"

"Nothing, Mack. I've checked everywhere to the left."

"Head back to the main room, stay close to the Wellman's – but don't alarm them. I don't want them knowing anything is amiss."

"Copy that."

I can trust Jack to be discreet – a hell of a lot more discreet than the other option at my disposal.

"Gilly, all clear on your end?" I ask.

No reply.

"Gilly," I bark into the small mic.

"Ah... Mack, I think you better get down here."

I'm back on the stairs before my brain even registers what I'm doing – I take the steps two at a time as I head back in the direction Gilly went.

"Where are you?" I hiss.

"Media room."

I jog down the hallway and turn around the bend, the door to the media room is just up ahead.

I burst through it and take in the scene in front of me.

Gilly has a woman backed up against a wall, his arms caging her in.

My eyes trail from her feet, up her silver glittery dress, all the way to her short black hair style.

"*Kinsley?*" I growl as I stride towards her. "What kind of fresh hell is this?"

CHAPTER TWENTY-TWO

Kinsley

Shit. Shit. *Shit*.

I should have known he'd find me – hunt me down like a dog with a bone.

I thought I could do this... put my feelings for him aside and do what I came here to do, but the minute he walked into the room and locked his brown eyes on mine, I was screwed.

He shifts his gaze from my face, to the man in front of me – the one who caught me red-handed, and tips his head.

Gilly, if I had to guess, smirks at me and steps back. "You're in trouble now, crazy."

I smirk back, trying my best to keep up the confident act that I'm not feeling in the slightest.

"What are you doing here?" Jared asks me, stepping closer as he does.

I want to answer him, I really do, but the words get caught in my throat.

I can see the disappointment in his eyes, and it hurts.

I hate that I've let him down, even if it was in an attempt to do the right thing.

Sometimes you don't know what you need – not until it's looking you right in the face.

And I know I need *him*.

More than need, I want him, and I haven't wanted anything for myself in a long time.

This isn't manipulation or games between us, this is real – for me at least – even though I'm screwing it all up by being here.

Gilly slides a chair out from the table, the legs dragging against the flooring and drops his body into it.

"She was tampering with the slide show, Mack," he tells Jared.

Jared glances at the open laptop on the table and then back to me.

"What the fuck, Kinsley? You made me a promise."

I reach for his arm, but he moves before I can touch him. "*Jared*," I plead, my voice a whisper.

He shakes his head. "Don't."

"This isn't about you... or us – it's just something I have to do," I whisper.

He laughs humourlessly. "Funny, because it sure as fuck feels like it's about us."

I feel my bottom lip tremble. I feel like I'm going to burst into tears.

"Here come the water works," Gilly drawls from his spot at the table.

I won't cry – not in front of them – if Jared won't forgive me after, I'll cry then. When I'm alone.

"It's pathetic really," Jared sneers, his eyes narrowing. "It was years ago that he fucked you, don't you think it's time you moved on?"

My eyes widen. "*Years?* Is that what he told you? Try a couple of *months*, big guy."

Jared and Gilly make eye contact for a beat. Gilly gets to his feet and comes to stand in front of me – next to his boss.

The two huge men stand shoulder to shoulder in front of me – both of their arms crossed against their chests.

"You're lying," Gilly accuses.

"I swear on my life, I slept with him a few months back."

"But what about Liana?" Jared eyes me cautiously.

"*Exactly*," I breathe. "Who the fuck do you think I've been trying to get to?"

Jared chuckles. "You're here for William, we all know that."

I huff out a breath. "You think I'm here for *him?*"

"If the 'stalker slipper' fits, Cinderella," Gilly chimes in.

"Oh please," I scoff. "He wasn't even a good lay."

The corner of Jared's mouth twitches. Gilly flat-out grins.

"So, you're trying to tell me that you slept with the boss only a couple of months ago – and you're here to tell Liana what? That her husband is a cheat?"

I pop a shoulder. "I'd probably use more colourful language, but sure, that's the gist of it."

Jared's arms tighten across his firm chest, and I have to restrain myself from reaching for him again.

I want to run my hands through his hair and kiss him until he stops looking at me the way he is now.

"Let's pretend that I believe everything you've told me... I have a question."

I arch a brow.

"Where'd he pick you up?"

I give Jared a coy smile. "Strip club."

His eyes darken. "Where'd he take you?"

"Fancy hotel downtown."

"Did you know who he was?"

I narrow my eyes. "I had no idea... not until after – the bastard lied about his name. I never would have knowingly slept with a married man – *or* my father's biggest business rival for that matter."

The two men glance at each other again, and they must have known each other a long time, because they're clearly having some type of silent conversation between them.

"Think about it..." I demand. "If I slept with him years ago, why would I have come back now all of a sudden?"

They exchange glances once more, but neither has an answer for me.

"I need a smoke," Jared says, his fingers massaging his temples.

"You don't smoke, boss," Gilly pipes up.

Jared shoots him a look before turning his focus back to me.

"What were you doing to the slide show?" he demands, his tone leaving no room for bullshit.

"Just adding in a few pictures..."

It's not what I wanted to do – embarrass Liana in front of all her friends and family, but I figure she'd thank me for it one day – this would ruin William and that's the best revenge she could hope for once she gets over the initial hurt.

Telling Liana is as much about taking a stand for me as it is for her – I'm tired of being used and swept under the rug by men.

I'm tired of being played.

If I say nothing, he gets away with it and she stays married to a jerk. I've tried to do this privately, but they've left me with limited options.

There's a girl code for crying out loud, and it's a real thing to me.

"Get her out of here," Jared says suddenly, and my already frantically beating heart speeds up again. "Hold her on the mezzanine level until I come back."

"Big guy, *please*, you have to believe me," I beg, my tone sounding frantic.

I reach for him as he turns, his attention shifting to the laptop on the table, but he's too far away.

He doesn't want my touch.

He doesn't even give me another glance as Gilly leads me out of the room.

***

"Sit." Gilly holds his hand out, gesturing for me to take a seat.

I do, my face falling into my hands.

This whole thing was for nothing. Jared will delete the security stills of William and I together, and Liana will still have no idea that she's married to a pig.

And on top of that – I've lost Jared – I really am just a crazy bitch in his mind now.

My minder sits down next to me after about ten minutes of pacing back and forth. "You know, I think Mack really likes you."

I huff out a laugh. "Maybe he did – but I've ruined all that now."

"Oh, I wouldn't be so sure…"

I roll my head to the side so I can look at him. He smirks and winks at me.

Poor Jared – he clearly attracts crazy company.

I open my mouth to say something, but Gilly shushes me.

"The show's about to start."

He points down to the floor below us, and across to the screen that is beginning to display the slideshow I tried and failed to hijack.

I roll my eyes. Pictures of William and Liana… That's *just* what I feel like watching.

CHAPTER TWENTY-THREE

Mack

"Mrs. Wellman, can I speak to you for a moment?"

She tips her head at me curiously.

I glance around, hoping that William isn't about to walk back in from wherever it is he's disappeared to.

"But the slideshow is about to start," she reminds me.

I nod my head. "I know. That's actually what I need to talk to you about... we have a problem."

I rest my hand on the small of her back and encourage her to come with me.

"Can't William sort it out?"

I look at her pointedly. "I think you'll want to handle this personally, Mrs. Wellman.... trust me."

Her brow furrows but she nods and follows me from the room.

***

"All good, boss?" Gilly's voice comes through my earpiece.

"Getting there," I reply as I make one final adjustment to the slide show.

Technology isn't exactly my favourite thing in the world – anniversary videos even less so, so I really hope I haven't fucked this up.

Kinsley had big plans for this show.

"Crazy fucking woman," I mutter under my breath.

"You still got her there with you?" I ask for the fifth time.

I doubt Kinsley could give him the slip, but who knows – she's resourceful.

"Copy that, Mack, all under control here."

"Jack?" I ask.

"In position, Mack – we're all just waiting on you to get this thing straightened out."

"I'm doing my damn best," I growl as the file finally finishes saving.

"Done," I announce.

"Virtual high-five." Gilly chuckles.

"I'm heading in the back to keep an eye on things."

"Copy that," they both reply.

I check the timer on the slide show once more, it's all pre-programmed to start at the right time, and I see it has two minutes to go before it goes live on the huge screen.

I've scraped in just in time.

I wipe the sweat from my brow – that felt like detonating a live bomb.

I leave the media room and head for the main room.

"If I can just have everybody's attention, we're about to play a short video slideshow – a collection of images showcasing the marriage of William and Liana," the MC for the evening announces to the room full of guests.

Everyone claps and the chatter in the room dies down as the lights dim in preparation.

I cross my arms and lean against the door frame to watch.

The huge screen on the far side flickers to life and I see William weaving through the crowd, heading back for the spot he left his wife.

Romantic music floats softly through the room as picture after picture from their wedding day is displayed on the screen.

There are pictures from their honeymoon, shots from their home – taken by some ridiculously overpriced photographer no doubt – and some more candid shots, snapped from Liana's cell phone by the looks.

The crowd laughs at a picture of William sleeping on the couch.

I catch sight of William in the crowd again, whispering in the ear of the blonde woman next to him.

Reminiscing about the old times perhaps...

I hear a collective gasp from the room, and I look up just in time to see the first of the shots that Kinsley had inserted into the slide show.

I grin to myself.

It's a very unforgiving position William has found himself in. He's riding in an elevator with a woman whose face we can't see, but one that is very clearly not his wife – the date and time stamp noticeable in the top corner.

He's got Kinsley pressed up against the wall, his hand pushing her dress further up her leg and her face buried in the crook of his neck – her dark hair spilling over her shoulder.

The image both turns me on and makes me want to punch something in the same moment.

It all clicked into place after Gilly took Kinsley away.

She was telling the truth.

Everything made sense. This whole time, she's been trying to get to *Liana*, not William.

She snuck into the yoga class... tried to get Liana away for a chat at the charity event...

I've been so blind.

The next image comes up – showing him undoing his belt and the crowd gasps again.

We still can't see Kinsley's face – I made sure that none of the photos gave away her identity. Only someone that's been as up close and personal with her as I have would ever know. And I'll make sure those pictures never see the light of day again after this evening.

"Oh my god," I hear someone cry as the next picture shows William with his pants around his ankles.

The blonde woman next to William – the one who isn't Liana, looks at him in disgust and storms off.

If I had to guess, I'd say he'd been doing something pretty similar with her only a few moments ago.

I chuckle and push off the wall, jogging down the hallway towards the stairs.

Instead of rushing up them, I take my time, being as quiet as I can in my approach.

Gilly turns when I reach the landing and gives me a thumbs up before tipping his head in the direction of Kinsley.

She's right at the front of the mezzanine, her back to me – she's watching the show.

"How'd I do?" I ask, and she freezes.

Her body turns, ever so slowly to face me.

"You believed me?" she asks, her eyes wide in disbelief.

"Of course I did. I just needed a minute to figure it all out."

"You finished what I started?"

I nod and take another step towards her. "I did."

"You *don't* think I'm crazy?"

I can see her eyes glossing over – she really thought I'd disregarded her so quickly.

Sure, I was hurt when I saw her here, but I'm not sure that would have been enough to erase her from my life – at this point, I'm not entirely sure I'd be capable of doing that.

I chuckle. "Woman, you are bat shit crazy, but it's what I love most about you."

Holy shit… did he say…

"Did he just drop the 'L' bomb?" Gilly chuckles.

"Shut up, Gilly," we both say in unison.

"Co-ordinated speech." He chuckles louder. "*Must* be love."

I close the distance between us and capture a strand of her newly cut hair between my fingers. "I like this… but what's with the sudden change?"

She shrugs. "I'm kind of unpredictable like that, you'll get used to it."

I smirk and tug her close, wrapping my arms around her tightly. "Yeah I will." I claim her lips, and she hums deep in her throat.

"This is such a sweet, *tender* moment," Gilly pipes up from behind me.

Kinsley giggles against my lips. "You were right – he *is* annoying."

"And I pride myself on it," he replies, and I can hear the grin in his voice. "I hate to be a buzz-kill, but Jack says it's time to go."

I grab Kinsley's hand in mine and tug her along next to me.

"Wait!" she exclaims suddenly, dragging her feet. "Liana wasn't down there – she didn't see it."

I pull on her arm again. "Trust me, she saw – I pulled her aside before the video – showed her the images and told her what you'd said – I didn't want her to be humiliated in public."

Kinsley squeezes my hand tighter as we descend the staircase. "So, you're telling me that all this time, I could have just shown you the pictures and told you he was an asshole, and you'd have taken care of the rest?"

"Would have made my life a hell of a lot easier," I growl. "But where's the fun in that?"

She giggles. "Why are we moving so fast? Some of us have heels on you know."

"Liana's waiting," Gilly explains, glancing over his shoulder at her.

"Waiting for *what*?"

It's my turn to explain now. "I pulled her aside right after you told me about Will – I told her what her husband had been doing behind closed doors... and then I made her an offer."

She raises her brows in question. "*Well*? Are you going to tell me what kind of offer?"

"I offered to be her head of security. She'll get fifty percent of William's net worth – she's a very wealthy woman – one who'll need her own security team."

"Oh my god. That is *so* savage." She smirks. "William is going to flip."

We make it out the exit, and I've got the door open to my four-wheel drive that Jack has pulled around front for us – that's when William finds us. I was hoping to get out of here without having to speak to him face to face, but it doesn't appear that luck is on my side tonight.

"Mack! What the fuck is going on?"

Gilly chuckles and skirts around me, heading for his own vehicle. "Good luck with that one, Mack."

Bastard.

Kinsley looks up at me with big wide eyes, and I nod my head, gesturing for her to climb in the front passenger's seat. Surprising absolutely nobody, she doesn't comply.

"What the fuck are you doing with her now?" he demands as he gets closer and sees who I'm trying to put in my car. "That little bitch ruined my life."

I cross my arms and plant my feet in the space between Kinsley and William, my stance protective.

He narrows his eyes at me. "You better be disposing of her."

I chuckle darkly. "Always so far behind, Wellman... the only person I'm disposing of, is *you*."

His jaw falls lax before he quickly regains composure and snaps it shut.

I don't know how he's made such a name for himself as a business shark, his poker face is terrible.

"You're on *my* payroll."

I chuckle darkly.

"You could say I'm... *transferring* my contract."

"You'll regret this," he snarls.

I plant my feet a little wider. "Regret *what*, exactly?"

"You'll regret it *all*... leaving me high and dry... bedding that slut... god knows *I* regret it."

I roll forward on the balls of my feet, I'm about to lunge forward and teach him a lesson for speaking about my woman that way when a small hand reaches around my middle, gripping my side.

I hear her soft voice at my ear. "He's not worth it, big guy."

I grind my teeth together – she's right, he's not worth it, but that doesn't make the idea of smashing his head in seem any less appealing.

"And where the hell is my wife?" he carries on, seemingly oblivious to the rage swirling within me and the fact that it's no longer my job to answer his questions.

That question gets a grin out of me though.

I'm about to tell him that he's lost it all when the rear window of my four-wheel drive slowly lowers.

"What do you want, William?" Liana asks, her tone bored.

I hear Kinsley gasp. I guess she wasn't aware that my new employer would be travelling with us.

"Liana?" William questions. "What are you doing in there?"

Credit to the woman, she's strong as hell – she doesn't even look upset, even though I know she's broken on the inside.

"Leaving you," she states simply. "And taking the security team with me... along with half of your money."

He turns a deep shade of purple.

"The 'no pre-nup' doesn't seem like such a good idea all of a sudden, does it, Will?" she taunts him.

The dumb bastard can't even speak; his mouth is opening and shutting like a goldfish.

"I'm ready to leave," Liana says, her voice lower, only for me to hear.

I nod at her and step further forward on the footpath so I can physically put Kinsley in her seat and shut the door.

"Two incredible women, William, and you chose to fuck them both over." I chuckle as I round the front of my car. "Guess you're not that smart after all."

Kinsley grins at me through the windscreen.

His loss, my gain.

CHAPTER TWENTY-FOUR

Kinsley

"Well... this is awkward." I lace and unlace my fingers in my lap.

Jared glances at me out the corner of his eye, his gaze drifting from my hands to my face and back again.

He reaches across the centre console and places his big hand over both of mine.

My nerves dissolve with just a simple touch from him.

He had my back in there, and again when William confronted us – he might have let me think he was going to be rid of me, but when push came to shove, he chose *me*.

I hope it's something he's going to make a habit of doing.

"Liana?" I say softly, unsure of how to address the woman whose marriage I played a part in ending.

"Yes...?"

"I just wanted to apologise... you know...for sleeping with your husband." I wince. "I swear I didn't know he was married."

"I doubt you were the first one... you probably weren't the last either." She sighs. "Good luck to wife number three, that's all I can say."

"You're not his first wife?"

"Nope."

"Huh," I muse.

The guy's only about mid-forties – pretty young to have a string of ex-wives.

"You really don't know?" she asks, and I frown.

"Know *what*?" I shake my head and look at Jared. He shrugs.

"William got married in his late twenties, and fairly early into the marriage, about fifteen years ago, he had an affair with a married woman."

So, he's got a habit of it then. Delightful.

"I'm not sure why you're telling me this..."

"It's the reason your father and my husband – *ex*-husband rather, hate each other so much."

The penny drops.

My mouth falls open. "*He* had an affair with *my* mother?"

"Well damn," Jared mutters. "That certainly explains the feud."

"I mean... I knew my mum cheated on my dad, but I had no idea that *William* was the guy..."

"He was the guy," she confirms. "I knew the story, but not the names until we ran into you and your father at that event."

Well shit.

"He told my dad about it, you know? My father never told me the man's name that came and confessed to the affair, but he said the guy was in love with my mother – that he thought they were going to live happily ever after, but she wasn't interested. I can't believe it was *him*... All this time, I thought they were just rivals in business."

"Business *and* the bedroom it would seem... *anyway*, I thought you should know... I thought the fact that Will was so open about his indiscretions and so remorseful meant that he'd learnt his lesson... that it wasn't something he planned on re-peating, but I guess I was wrong."

"I'm sorry."

"Don't be. He's a pig."

He certainly fucking is.

"I'm just glad I know now."

That was all I ever wanted. I'm glad Liana doesn't seem to hate me – so many people blame the woman in these situations, but I wouldn't care if she did. She finally knows the truth and that's the most important thing – what she does with it is up to her.

"*Ew.*" I scrunch up my nose as I think again about this new snippet of information. "I slept with the same man as my mother."

That is possibly the grossest sentence I've ever had to utter.

"Promise me no one will tell Gilly about this, he has this strange fascination with sleeping with a mother and then her daughter." Jared shakes his head at his friend's antics.

"He's a truly disturbed individual."

"This is like that movie where three generations sleep with the same dude." He chuckles before his smirk drops, and a frown replaces it. "If we ever have a daughter, she is *never* going anywhere near that prick."

"Did you just talk *children*? Now who's letting their crazy show?" I gape.

A deep chuckle rumbles in his chest.

"Christ, *big guy*," I shake my head at him. "At least make me a wife before you start thinking about renting out my uterus."

"Noted."

"You two are quite strange, in case you weren't already aware..." Liana informs us.

"She brings it out in me, sorry, boss – we'll keep it more professional from now on." Jared glances at her in his rear-view mirror. "And for what it's worth, I'm really sorry he hurt you – you deserve a lot better than William Wellman."

"Don't. I kind of like strange," she replies. "And thank you, I certainly do."

I squeeze Jared's hand and grin at him.

I can't believe this is finally over.

I don't know what I'll do with all my spare time now that I can cross stalking off the list.

"I just have one more question..." Liana probes.

"Okay..."

"What the hell is a girl like you doing dancing in a strip club?"

Before I even get the chance to explain that it was just for inspiration, the big guy cuts in and answers for me. "It doesn't matter why," he growls. "The only thing you need to know is she's done with it."

"Am I now?" I ask, brows raised.

"You bet your ass you are. I don't need to be breaking dude's noses, and you don't need any more god damn sex appeal, that's for *damn* sure."

I don't know if I hate the fact that he just spoke on my behalf, or if I really freakin' like it.

I don't know who I think I'm kidding – I *definitely* like it.

"Breaking noses, huh?" I ask with a giggle.

He smirks. "Wouldn't even feel bad about it. But you're welcome to practise on me, at home, any god damn time you like, baby."

He pulls up outside a hotel that would cost more per night than some people make in an entire week.

"Gilly and Jack will be at your beck and call, Ms. Wellman," Jared tells his new boss, turning in his seat to face her.

"Call me Liana or you're fired."

He chuckles. "Liana, then."

"We'll get together tomorrow and make a plan for the removal of your things from the house."

"Excellent." She yawns. "Now if you'll excuse me... that was quite the night."

"That's an understatement," I mutter under my breath.

"You don't happen to know any handsome, single men my age?" Liana asks as she unclips her belt.

Jared chuckles.

I grin to myself, I know she's joking, but as luck would have it, I know just the man – I'll have to tuck that idea away for a more appropriate time.

The back door swings open and Gilly's smiling face appears. "You ready, boss 2.0?"

She puts her hand in his and he helps her from the car before sticking her head back in to speak to the man next to me.

"Thank you, Mack... for being discreet, and for your loyalty to me – it hasn't gone unnoticed."

Jared tips his head to her in response and then she's gone, and we're driving around the darkened streets once again.

"Where to now then?"

"Home," he replies simply.

"You sure you still want me after you've seen all of my crazy?"

He chuckles and his hand slides onto my thigh through the split in my dress. "Does it make me stupid for wanting you even more?"

"It makes me concerned for your mental state..."

He slides his phone from his pocket and hands it to me. "Call your father, tell him you won't be home for quite some time."

I take the phone from him, biting my lip as I do. "What if he asks why I haven't packed any clothes?"

He chuckles. "Then you can tell him your new boyfriend said you won't need any."

"Ooooh, *boyfriend*... snuck that one in there, didn't ya?"

I grin as I dial my father's number – not his head of security this time. I could use my own phone, but there's something about the call coming from Jared's phone that sends a distinct message.

"I got sick of being called a kidnapper." He shrugs, his expression amused as he heads across town to his place. "Had to get myself a new title."

It's a title I can live with.

"Kent Barlett speaking," my father answers his phone, business as always.

"Hey, Daddy."

"*Kinsley*?" he asks in confusion. As far as he's aware – I went to bed hours ago.

"It's me," I confirm. "I decided to go out."

"*Without* security?" he demands.

"I've got the only security I need, Daddy, but he's not on your payroll."

"Name," he demands, and I can hear him pacing the room.

I glance over at Jared and he nods, letting me know he can hear and he's okay with being thrown to the wolves.

"Jared McKenzie."

I hear my father repeat the name – to someone on his team no doubt. They should have any information that Jared has been willing to make available, in their hot little hands within about thirty seconds.

"I worked with Mack, sir, he's a good guy," I hear someone tell my father in the background.

"This *Mack*," he questions, speaking to me now, "are you spending time with him for business or pleasure?"

"Definitely pleasure," Jared speaks before I can.

My dad groans, having heard him.

"Sorry, Daddy, maybe don't ask questions if you don't want to hear the answers to them?"

He's quiet for a few beats.

"Can he take care of you, darling?"

I nibble on my lip nervously.

"Ask your boy in the background, see what he thinks."

He does as I suggest, and I hear him ask, "Can this guy take care of my daughter?"

"I don't want to get fired or anything here, sir, but he could look after her one hundred times better than I ever could."

I risk a glance at the man next to me and his chest is puffed out so far I'm concerned it might pop.

I roll my eyes.

"*One hundred times better?* What exactly am I paying you for then?" he demands.

"Daddy," I interrupt. "Can we wrap this up? I've got things to do."

"Are you sure about this?"

Jared's hand rubs my thigh reassuringly.

"I'm sure about a lot of things, Daddy. I think it might be time we had an honest conversation about what I want from my life."

He's silent for a few beats. "I guess I knew this day would come... Monica is always telling me that I couldn't keep you stuck here forever."

"So why did you try?" I ask with a sigh as Jared pulls up to the garage door that will take us into his huge lift.

"You're my little girl," he replies simply.

I'm not a little girl at all anymore, but I appreciate the sentiment, and decide that this is a conversation that can wait for another time.

"I've got to go."

"Alright. You call me if you need anything, okay, anytime..."

"I will."

"I want to meet this man... and don't think we won't be having words about how you've found yourself shacked up with William Wellman's head of security."

"Of course," I reply with a wary sigh. "Goodnight, Daddy."

"Goodnight, darling."

"I want everything there is to know about Jared McKenzie, and I want it yesterday!" I hear him demand before the line goes dead.

We're down on the level of Jared's home now, and I hand him back his phone with a wince. "You're probably going to regret the moment you ever laid eyes on me, big guy."

His hand slides further up my thigh. "I doubt that very much, baby. You're not someone I'm *ever* going to regret."

CHAPTER TWENTY-FIVE

Mack

"Are you sure you're ready for this? It's a hell of a lot more scary than dealing with some crazy bitch stalking your boss." She grins at me, her eyes sparkling.

I chuckle but grip her hand a little tighter. "I handled you, didn't I?"

"I'm not sure you'll be able to use the same techniques. I doubt my father will respond well to being pressed against a wall and seduced."

"He doesn't know what he's missing."

She shakes her head in amusement and smoothes down her top.

"Monica will be out in a second, are you ready?"

"Am I ready to meet my girlfriend's billionaire father who is the rival of my ex-boss? I mean sure, just a quiet Sunday, right?"

She tips her head back and laughs freely.

I love when she does that.

I just love *her* to be honest. That's why I'm here, wearing a fucking suit that I can't stand, about to have dinner with one of the most powerful men in the world, and somehow navigate a conversation about my intentions with his little girl.

Just a standard day at the office.

I tug on my collar – it suddenly feels too tight.

Kinsley swats my hand away. "Stop fussing, you look good enough to eat."

"Maybe that's what I'm afraid of," I mutter as the door opens in front of us and a sweet-looking older woman's smiling face appears.

"Miss Barlett." She grins. "It's been quiet without you."

"Hey, Mon." She gestures to me. "This is Jared, but you can call him Mack."

"Mr. McKenzie." She nods in my direction, and I see Kinsley roll her eyes out of my peripherals. "I've heard a lot about you."

She shouldn't have – considering Kinsley hasn't set foot inside this house since her father learnt my name – but no doubt Kent has had his team on the case, digging around into my past, all too eager to find out who has stolen away his prized daughter.

"I've heard a lot about you too," I say as I slip my arm around Kinsley's waist and tug her against me.

Monica watches the action with fondness, her eyes softening as Kinsley pushes up to her tip toes and kisses my jaw.

"Is Daddy ready for us?"

"He's waiting in the formal dining." She ushers us inside, takes our coats and hangs them up before disappearing.

"Is it wrong that I get a little bit turned on when you say the word 'daddy'?" I ask in a hushed voice as Kinsley leads me through a grand foyer and into what looks like a formal living room.

"It's wrong on *so* many levels, big guy.

I chuckle.

"You better stop talking before I can't look my father in the eye ever again."

We step into the dining room and about a dozen sets of eyes cut to us.

I reach up to straighten my tie and Kinsley giggles.

She tugs my hand down and holds it in hers.

I glance down at her and those crystal blue eyes melt me.

I'd go through hell for this woman – a meal with her father and his friends will be a walk in the park.

Kent stands as we approach, and Kinsley skips over to him, her sleek black bob bouncing.

Her father takes her in his arms and hugs her before holding her at arm's length and touching the ends of her hair. "Do you think you'll ever go more than two weeks without changing this hair?"

Kinsley pops a shoulder. "Probably not."

She shrugs off her father's hands and turns back, reaching for me.

I take her hand in mine and step forward to meet her father – the most important man in her life – at least until I came along.

"Daddy, this is Jared McKenzie, Jared, this is my dad, Kent."

I extend my hand to him. "It's good to officially meet you, Mr. Barlett."

He grips my hand in his and shakes it firmly.

"So, you're the man who's managed to steal my daughter's heart?"

"Couldn't tell you, sir... she keeps her cards fairly close to her chest."

He chuckles and drops my hand. "I've taught her well."

Kinsley narrows her eyes at her father. "If you keep letting him call you such formal names, we're going to have a problem, Daddy."

He studies his daughter for a few beats, and whatever he sees obviously works.

"Please, Mack, sit… and call me Kent."

I pull out a chair for Kinsley and take the vacant one next to her.

She grips my leg under the table and leans in to my ear. "You stole my heart, big guy, I think you've owned it since the first time you threw me over your shoulder."

"I'm glad to hear that, would have made the question I have to ask your father pretty awkward otherwise."

She furrows her brow and opens her mouth to question what I'm talking about, but her dad starts making introductions to the rest of the table, effectively cutting her off.

"So, Jared, Kent tells me you run security for William Wellman?" the guy down the end of the table whose name I missed, asks me.

"I did," I reply as Monica places a small plate of food in front of me. I smile at her in thanks. "But I've very recently shifted my team and our employment to Liana Wellman – William's very recently *ex*-wife."

Kent's eyes light up with interest. "Oh? I hadn't heard."

Kinsley nods her head. "He cheated… can you imagine that, Daddy?" She stares at him pointedly, letting him know that she's in on the little secret, and that she's not particularly impressed about being left in the dark.

"Is that so..." Kent muses, a smirk on his lips as he lifts his glass.

"Certainly is," she replies with a smirk of her own as she brings a forkful of food to her mouth.

"You know what, Daddy, you should send some flowers and a note over to Liana, I'm sure she'd appreciate knowing that your feud with her ex-husband doesn't extend to her."

He nods his head slowly as he contemplates it. "I might just do that, darling."

Kinsley's eyes sparkle deviously – my woman looks like she's up to no good and I can't think of anything better.

"So... *Kinsley*, what are your plans for the remainder of the year?" the woman across from her asks – I think her name was Sandra.

Kinsley's eyes dart to her father. I lay my hand over hers on the top of the table.

I've got her back – with *anything* she wants to do.

I'm pretty confident I know exactly what that is – if all the talking she's done over the past few days is anything to go by.

She glances at our hands and smiles up at me gratefully. "I've actually been dancing a lot. I've been working with a really talented local group and I'm looking to get into doing more choreography this year."

"That sounds fantastic, are you still dancing ballet?"

"Not exactly." Kinsley tightens her grip on my hand. "I've been more into hip hop and freestyle for a while now."

She faces her father, who is looking at her in surprise.

The table falls silent for a moment; it seems everyone is waiting to see how Kent reacts to his daughter's confession.

It's obvious, even to me, that this group of people do a lot of things simply for appearances – Kinsley included.

"My niece is part of a group that danced in a Justin Bieber music video," the guy down the end who spoke to me earlier pipes up. "She's doing incredibly well. I hear it's a booming industry."

It's a total wanker rich-guy comment, but I can forgive his pompous ass for making it, because it's clear his intention is to break the ice and support my girl, and that makes him alright by me.

"Hip hop?" Kent asks Kinsley, his voice quiet. "What happened to ballet? You were so good, darling."

She shrugs. "I was... I still am. But I don't feel ballet in my soul the same way I feel my other dancing."

He looks a little bit shaken, so I hope to god he doesn't ever find out about the half-naked dancing she was doing in the strip club – the guy might have a heart attack.

He sips his drink and studies her. "And you're happy?"

She nods.

"Well, then I guess it's alright by me." He nods, convincing himself more than anyone else if I had to guess. "And if it's a booming industry..."

He turns to his guests and they carry on having their douche conversation that's all about money.

Kinsley squeezes my hand, and I grin at her. "You've got this, baby."

***

"So... *Mack*," Kent says over the rim of the glass that never seems to be far away, "What exactly are your plans for my daughter?"

I watch Kinsley as she laughs with Monica across the room – the woman she told me she sees as a surrogate mother or grandmother.

We're off to the side to have a private word.

I've been summoned to the bar to get the 'dad talk'.

"With all due respect, sir, I wouldn't bother making plans when it comes to a woman like Kinsley – she's unpredictable and she certainly likes to keep me on my toes, so if it's alright with you, I think I'll just take things as they come."

He tips his glass at me. "I heard you were a smart man."

"But there *is* one thing I wanted to ask."

"The floor is yours." He takes another sip of his drink as he waits for me to speak.

"I'd like permission to marry your daughter."

He almost spits out the mouthful he just took. "Jesus Christ, I thought you just said you were going to see how things went?"

I nod. "I am. I'm not going to marry her yet, but one day – you can bet I fucking am. Nothing is going to change that fact, so I figure I may as well get the formality out of the way now."

"A straight shooter," he comments. "I guess I can appreciate that."

"So is that a yes or a no?" I probe.

He points at his daughter. "You keep making her happy – keep her out of trouble, and we're good."

I'm not sure I can promise the latter, but I'm not about to tell him that.

I raise my glass, and he clinks his against it.
Kent Barlett. My future father-in-law.
Who the hell would have thought?

EPILOGUE

Mack

"You know, when I thought I'd play match maker six months ago, I never thought that it'd all work out and they'd actually get *married*."

I chuckle. "Well, baby, sometimes when two people love each other—"

"Oh, shut up," she interrupts me, smacking her hand against my chest, the gesture more affectionate than it is scolding.

I grin at her, my little fruit loop. She's still as crazy as she was the day we met over a year ago, but if anything, I only love her more for it.

"Daddy wants me to try some cake samples and Liana needs me to have another stupid dress fitting." She pouts.

"You're starting to sound like you hate weddings."

She narrows her eyes at me. "I wouldn't hate *my own* wedding, but you haven't married me yet, so..."

I chuckle louder. "Is that so?"

I slide my hand into my pocket and check for the one hundredth time that the damn ring box is still where I left it.

Give me a billionaire to protect and I'm confident – any damn day of the week – but give me a family heirloom ring to keep safe, and I'm a nervous wreck.

"What are you doing here anyway, can't you see I'm working?" she replies, her tone sassy.

I know she's really thrilled I'm here on set to see her work. She's killing it.

"Just wanted to see you in action, baby, you know how much I appreciate it when you shake that ass."

She rolls her eyes, a smirk on her lips.

"Well, you'll have to sit here quietly, break's almost over, big guy."

She goes to stroll away, back onto the set, but I grab her arm and tug her roughly so her chest collides against mine with a thud. "You look smokin', did I tell you that already?" I growl against her lips.

"Twice," she breathes.

I press my lips to hers and kiss her long and hard.

"Get a room," a male voice calls.

I chuckle. "I still *really* fucking hate Robbo."

She giggles and pops a shoulder. "Kid's got mad skills though..."

She pulls away from me, and I smack her on the ass as she goes, just in case she forgot who that sexy rear of hers belongs to.

I watch as she rallies around her dancers – the same ones I watched perform in the street all those months ago, her best friend Courtney included, and they huddle up tight.

She's come such a long way since I first met her – from the woman lying about her passion and pretending to dance ballet, to a bad-ass hip hop choreographer who, along with her crew, is highly sought after by some of the world's biggest artists and brands.

I've come a long way too – from working for a wanker to being employed by his ex-wife and, given that she's marrying my girlfriend's father in a little over two weeks – I'm in turn now employed by Kent Barlett as well.

His head of security didn't last long once I found out he'd had sex with the woman I share a bed with every night – so this arrangement Kent and I have come to, works out well for everyone.

I get more time with my girl, and her father rests easy knowing that she has me there to protect her – forever.

I hit dial on Gilly's name on my phone and bring it up to my ear as I watch Kinsley going through a couple of moves with one of the girls and then getting everyone into position.

"What's up, boss?" he answers.

"Is everything going to plan?"

"Course it is."

"You sure you haven't fucked it all up?"

"Oh, ye of little faith."

"Just answer the question, Gilly."

He laughs. "Yeah, yeah. Everything is in position, *Romeo*. I gotta say, man, I didn't know you had it in you to be so... *cute*."

I close my eyes and shake my head in exasperation. I should have had Tom or Jack do this for me – I should have known better than to have Gilly help me set up the scene for my proposal to Kinsley, yet, somehow, I didn't.

I guess I'm a sucker for punishment.

"Thanks, Gilly. Now get the hell out of my house."

"Right after I light the candles and take a romantic bath," he taunts me.

"Gilly, I swear to fucking god, if I come home and you're in the bath, I'll kill you. I know people – no one would ever find your body."

"I don't doubt that, boss," he answers, and I can hear him using my god damn coffee machine. "I'll be out once I finish my mocha."

"You're such a girl."

"Coming from the dude with flowers and candles all over his bachelor pad."

"Not a bachelor pad, Gill, hasn't been for about eight months now."

He chuckles. "Gotta go, Mack, the sweet aroma of my chocolaty coffee is tempting me."

"Fuck's sake. Don't make a mess," I groan.

"Aye aye, captain. Tell Kinsley I say congratulations." He chuckles before hanging up.

"Idiot," I mutter to myself. For someone that insisted I was crazy for being with her in the first place, he's awful damn fond of her these days.

"Frustrating work call?" a guy holding a camera asks me.

"Something like that," I reply as I tuck my phone away.

"You're Mack, right? Kinsley's boyfriend?"

I nod and extend my hand to him. "And you are?"

He shakes my hand. "Ryan. I'm just the camera guy."

"You working on the shoot?"

He nods. "I hope you don't mind – this is kinda left field.... but I snapped a bunch of shots the other day and you were in some of them – anyway... a client that I'm working with for another project saw you and asked me to give you her card."

He hands me a business card.

I frown in confusion but take it from his outstretched hand. "Is she looking for a security guy?"

He grins. "Sort of."

I raise my brows at him in question. "You're not giving me much here, man, what does this woman want?"

"She runs a sexy, shirtless-man calendar... you know the type, and in her words, you'd be a perfect 'captivating body-guard.'"

"Come again?"

He shrugs. "Apparently she was captivated."

I laugh loudly. "You're kidding, *right*?"

"Afraid not." He chuckles. "But you should call her... I get a bonus if you do."

"Shameless self promotion, I can live with that." I chuckle.

I tuck the card into my pocket, even though I'm confident I won't be calling that number anytime soon.

"I gotta get back to work, but I thought you should know that Kinsley is all kinds of keen to get you signed up for it."

He walks off, huge camera in his hand, chuckling.

I catch Kinsley's eye and she's grinning, a huge shit-eating grin.

"Wait, *what*?" I call after him when it registers what he said.

He doesn't turn.

"Shit," I mutter to myself as I narrow my eyes at Kinsley.

This *fucking* woman.

OTHER TITLES

Love like Yours Series
Rushed – Book 1
Pierced – Book 2
Hunted – Book 3
Chased – Book 4

Rock Games Novels
Paper, Scissors, Rock: Vol. 1
Hide and Seek: Vol. 2

My Heart Duet
My Heart Needs
My Heart Wants

Calendar Boys Novels
Mr. January
Mr. February
Mr. March
Mr. April
Mr. May
Mr. June

ACKNOWLEDGEMENTS

The songs that inspired this book – *Maneater* – Nelly Furtado and *Sweet but Psycho* – Ava Max.

This book marks the halfway point in this series, and I'm still having so much fun with it. I love hearing what you think – so to those of you reading – thank you so much!

My editors, Stacey and Trina, who put up with me and my non-existent deadlines and timeframes, and also my inability to figure out if it should be a capital letter or a lowercase after speech – sorry about that! Thanks for all your hard work.

Bianca, Lauriel, Marnie, Trish, Kylee, Karen, Kath, Marg, Robyn and all the girls in my street team and reader group who also read for me before release, thank you so much for letting me know any mistakes you spot and for loving my characters with me. You're the best!

ABOUT THE AUTHOR

NICOLE S. GOODIN is a romance author and mother of two from Taranaki in the North Island of New Zealand.

In mid-2015, she started to write about a group of characters who wouldn't get out of her head. Her first book, Rushed, was published in mid-2016.

Nicole enjoys long walks on the beach, pillow fights and braiding her friends' hair. She dislikes clichés, talking about herself in the third person, and people who don't understand her sense of humour.

Please feel free to contact her either via her website, email, Instagram, Twitter or on her Facebook page, she would love to hear your feedback. If you're feeling really game, you can even sign up for her newsletter.

Visit www.nicolegoodinauthor.com for more information.

UPCOMING TITLES

Calendar Boys Novels

Mr. July
Mr. August
Mr. September
Mr. October
Mr. November
Mr. December